Hitting The High Note

A Four Horsemen Novel

By

C. A. King

Cover Design: Ravenborn Covers

Editor: **Karen Hrdlicka**

This book is dedicated to my readers. Without you,

my novels would be nothing more than words on a blank page.

-and-

To the people who have never given up on me, even in the rough times!

Look for other books by C.A. King, including:

The Portal Prophecies Series

Tomoiya's Story

Surviving the Sins

When Leaves Fall: A Different Point of View Story

Peach Coloured Daisies: A Cursed by the Gods Story

Flower Shields: A Four Horsemen Novel

Drawing Strength from Words: A Four Horsemen Novel

Miracles Not Included

Twisted Tales of A Dead End Street

Shot Through The Heart: A Faerie Tale

Welcome to Knollville Series

Tails Always Wins

Sometimes Love Stinks

Cupid's Connection

Cover Design: Ravenborn Covers

First Printing: June 2019

Second: August 2019

ISBN: 978-1-988301-81-5

Kings Toe Publishing

kingstoepublishing@gmail.com

Burlington, Ontario. Canada

Opening Thoughts

Creation. Over the years, there have been hundreds of plausible explanations for how and why man came into being. The problem that has plagued an entire race throughout the ages was and always will be which of these interpretations, if any, held truth?

Humans have always required knowledge. Where did they come from? Why were they put here? This whole species has searched for explanations locked somewhere in the limits of their own minds. Imagination itself held the key to opening the door. Once unlocked, the possibilities were endless. Myths and legends were born and passed down through the ages.

A simple recanting of these stories has, without question, revealed proof of a common thread between them. Few would argue that, at the root of most origin tales, there existed the acknowledgement of the presence of one or more supreme beings – someone or thing credited for having brought about all life on earth. Where these celestial beings, referred to as gods, came from may never be known. If, however, one knew where to look, one could find evidence of their time here – or perhaps the scars they left behind.

The following was one of those stories – a love story gone wrong.

Prologue

In a place where creativity through art, dance, poetry, and music was coveted above all else, a child was born. From the very beginning, Ihenna was thought of as by far the most beautiful of her kind. In a realm mesmerized by refinement, it was of no surprise to anyone, when she came of age to take a mate, suitors lined up with unimaginable gifts to win her hand and her heart.

It was Nakamire who won in the end. His admiration for Ihenna was unmatched. Of course, when he presented his gift, he had no idea one of his nine brothers was in the line behind him. Zahare never had the opportunity to profess his love, though it wouldn't have mattered if he did. Nothing could compare to Nakamire's creation – a world filled with beauty, born from pure love.

This new world was designed in two levels. One, in the open, where plants and animals roamed free, and another below, where his bride-to-be could escape to if she became overwhelmed by her surroundings.

It was the surface Ihenna fell in love with. Enough so that she decided to make it her home. A grand castle was built, surrounded by stunning gardens filled with her favourite flowers. It was a temple for his bride-to-be that captured everything she held in high regard. Her future husband had attended to every detail, including the race of man to admire her. They showered her with beautiful words, art, and music. Her life was a dream world where only the things she loved most existed.

Being worshipped as a god had a certain undeniable appeal. Nakamire's siblings and friends quickly joined the proud couple, eager to stay in paradise and share in the abundance of happiness – albeit some relished their newfound roles a little too much. A new race of demigods was born, carrying the bloodlines of both the creator and creation.

Unbeknownst to them, not everyone shared in their bliss. Every day Zahare witnessed their love, he grew more bitter, eventually taking up residence alone below the surface world. Blatant attempts to fill the growing void inside him with numerous women failed. A race of half-breeds born from jealousy and rage were his only reward.

Zahare despised this new world. His own offspring became his personal demons – twisting his consciousness further into the depths of insanity. It was there, in the lunacy of his own mind, a plan took life. He would kill Nakamire and take Ihenna for himself.

Fuelled by the words of a madman, his demons embraced the power each inherited – their only goal to be the one to sit by their father's side and win his approval.

When the day came, Zahare approached his brother, deception dancing on his lips in the form of a smile – a poisoned dagger concealed. One prearranged distraction was all he needed to unsheathe his weapon and, with every ounce of anger he had stored, plunge it deep into flesh.

It was over in a flash, but it wasn't Nakamire who lay lifeless on the marble floor. Ihenna used her own body to block the attack. Zahare killed the only woman he had ever loved. Screams of anguish by not one, but two, gods rumbled through the skies, quaking the earth.

If Zahare hadn't been consumed by madness before, he was now. Blaming not only his brother, but also the race of man and the world they lived in, he called forth his strongest demons to unleash their powers born from his rage: pestilence; famine; war; and death. Demanding total destruction, he promised to take the most loyal of his spawn to another world – one ruled by darkness.

Nakamire had lost his true love, but he wasn't about to let the world she held so dear suffer the same fate. With half-breeds by his side, a battle like no other ensued. The others, Nakamire's friends and family, once thought of as mighty gods, fled, refusing to be caught in the wake of certain destruction. They were, in fact, on the verge of being prophetic.

Heavy casualties were suffered on both sides. In the end, only one could win. Nakamire and the demigods stood victorious, but on that day, there were no feasts or celebrations.

With all he had already lost, Nakamire couldn't bear to destroy his brother as well. Instead, he sealed Zahare, and as many of his brother's demon offspring as could be found beneath the surface world – a jail meant to provide a constant reminder of the atrocities that had been committed. Four locked gates stood between the two plateaus. One demigod was chosen as protector of each gate, should Zahare ever find a way to open them.

In the wake of devastation, Nakamire tried to rebuild – hoping to bask in the memory of Ihenna's happiness. Like so many others, he too turned to female companionship, attempting to fill the void. By the time he realized his mistake, he had already become a father many times over. Unlike the other gods, however, he felt a connection to these demigods. Torn between an inability to remain in mourning and his love for his children, Nakamire was forced to make a choice. With heavy heart, he left his creation, allowing only those born of his world to return with him. Zahare, the demons, and the demigods were all left behind. That day the gate to the heavens was destroyed, never to open again.

*****

Over time, truths became legends – merely tales passed down from generation to generation. Slowly, the facts mutated – a little sensationalism added at a time – until only a thread of authenticity remained.

Demigods and demons alike disappeared. Records of their existence were destroyed. What once was became little more than the whispers of secret organizations. They, however, weren't gone, but were merely lying in wait, to one day appear again.

The guardians of the four gates remained faithful to their cause through the ages – seeking out and destroying demons trying to free their forefather from the confines of the hell he had been sentenced to live in.

Thousands of years later, a new threat appeared on the horizon...

Chapter One

Dante poured himself a double shot of whisky. It slid down his throat, burning a trail from mouth to stomach. He shuddered at the taste, glancing at the label on the bottle. It wasn't the spirit's fault, although it lacked the depth of character he preferred. The company he was in was to blame. That was what made such a drink a pleasurable experience.

"A bit early for alcohol, isn't it?" Creta squawked.

"That's a matter of opinion," Dante replied, pouring another, even if the taste was as bitter as the sight of his third wife. Keeping his back facing her didn't stop memories of her thick, stone-grey skin etched with wrinkles and scars.

"My opinion says it is," Creta blurted out.

His wooden desk begged for mercy beneath the pressure of a single fingernail. The scraping noise was simply more torture to add to a long list he kept tally of deep within his mind.

"Must you do that?" Dante complained.

"You know I'm at a disadvantage since my wings were clipped by that horseman and his flower girl. Besides, if you paid proper attention to your wives, I wouldn't have to," Creta argued.

"This is why we can't have nice things," Dante scoffed, turning around. He pointed to the gouges in the wood.

"You can buy whatever you want," Creta hissed. "This piece of junk can be replaced a thousand times over."

"It's an antique," Dante replied. "I don't expect you to understand the value of such things, but surely you can grasp the concept of it being aged and irreplaceable."

"You bore me with your relics," Creta scoffed. "They are nothing more than souvenirs of a world long lost. Those days are gone for a reason."

"Maybe it would be better if they still existed," Dante argued. "Things were built better back then. There was quality behind the work, rather than a mass production of items meant to appease the out-of-control population." He leaned back in his chair, polished black shoes, hitting the desktop. "Don't judge me." He shook his head. "You've already ruined it. My feet can't make things any worse."

"You haven't said a thing about my appearance," Creta complained. "I thought you might like a change. What do you think? Does this form appeal to you?" She spun around in a circle.

"There's another five years before you are fertile again," Dante replied. The glass pressed to his lips, stopping further words from escaping.

"I was hoping we could play," Creta cooed, rounding his desk and chair. Her hands reach over his shoulders, playing with the buttons on his shirt. "Don't you fancy a little pain and a lot of pleasure? I can offer you both."

"Not really," Dante said, pulling away from her grasp. "I never enjoyed women who spent a few too many hours in the plastic surgeon's office."

Creta cupped her breasts. "Too big?"

"Much," Dante replied, rolling his eyes.

"Tell me what you want, then," Creta begged. "I can be anything you desire. A redhead with large hips, perhaps? I can be exactly what you want."

"I doubt that," Dante mumbled under his breath. The sound of rapping on the door hid his response. "Come in." Any visitor was a welcome distraction.

"Sir," a man said, standing at attention before them. " I received a message that you wanted to see me."

"Have you located the artifact yet?" Dante questioned, eyeing the man up and down. "Or a line on our third key?"

"No, sir," the man answered. His hands remained folded behind his back. Beads of sweat formed on his brow – proof of his guilt. Wandering eyes kept Creta's ample bosom in view. He reeled in his drool before attempting to speak again. "We believe the item is being stored in a place that protects it from being traced. The moment it is in the open, we will know."

Dante leaned back, twiddling his thumbs. "It's Carl, isn't it? Tell me, Carl, do like my wife?"

"Sir?!" Carl stuttered.

"Do you enjoy the way my wife looks?" Dante questioned. "Do you find her attractive?" He stood, rounding the desk. "They aren't difficult questions to answer. Take a good look." Creta's new form posed seductively.

The man's gaze alternated between the two. "She's a very attractive woman, sir," he answered. "You are a lucky man."

"Excellent!" Dante exclaimed, clasping his hands together. "Since you failed to fulfill your current duties, I am reassigning you."

"Reassigning, sir?" Carl echoed. "I'm not sure I follow."

Creta circled the man, glancing over every inch. One hand grazed over his shoulders. "What a wonderful idea," she cackled.

"Very good," Dante said. "You have your new play toy. Take him away and do what you must. Send in a replacement for him on your way out. Oh, and, Carl, I wouldn't look directly into her eyes. Those black pits of ooze can affect a man's sanity." A coy smile formed in the corners of his lips. "Trust me, I'd know." He tossed back the remainder of his drink.

The man's eyes widened, curious as to what had happened. He stumbled, Creta's grip on one arm tugging him along behind her. Another man appeared in the doorway a moment later.

"Ah good," Dante said. "I need you to take over for Carl. He won't be in any condition to..." he shrugged his shoulders, "do much of anything for a long time. What's your name?"

"Dean, sir. How can I serve?"

"Find a way to bring the artifact and the third key into the open," Dante ordered. "We need to locate them before anyone else does. Understood?"

"Yes, sir," Dean answered.

"Well," Dante said. "What are you waiting for? Go!"

"How, exactly, did you want me to do that?" Dean questioned, his brows forming peaks, before crashing down into a frown.

"I don't know," Dante bellowed. "Take out an ad in a paper for all I care. Just get me results or you could end up one of Creta's play toys too. Trust me, you won't like that. You have forty-eight hours to show me progress."

"Understood, sir." The man scurried out the door.

Dante tapped his fingers on his desk. The new damage meant renovations were in order. Perhaps it was time for a new look – one that would suit the room after his plans were completed. Things were progressing as he anticipated, after all, and ahead of schedule. It wouldn't be long now. The top drawer squeaked open. A picture stared back at him. He ran his fingers over each person's image, saying their names out loud.

"Michael, Gabrielle, Uriel, and Raphael," he sighed, slamming the drawer shut. "You'll soon understand."

Chapter Two

A string of robberies left Bekka no choice. She wasn't the only thing in the music supply store that was fourth generation; the alarm was, too. It had to be updated. The worker installing it glanced over his shoulder; unnerved by the hole her glares were burning in the back of his uniform. She had no intention of blinking, either. This system cost more than she could afford, and did considerably less than was needed. State-of-the-art anything wasn't made for family businesses, especially when the family consisted of one person.

Bekka had been brought up in that very store, providing her with a strong appreciation of music. A future without the shop didn't seem possible – even if her dream was to, one day, play in an orchestra. Of course, there wasn't much chance of that happening. Practice might have made perfect, but it didn't matter if nobody ever heard that perfection.

"All done," the installer said, brushing his palms against each other. "You press your code and then have thirty seconds to leave the premises. When you open, unlock the door, and you have thirty seconds to input your code."

"Thirty seconds!" Bekka exclaimed, counting on her fingers how long it took to get the keys out of the door and the coffee cup rim from between her teeth. "That's not a lot of time." She scurried after him.

"It's pretty standard," the man said, trying to make his escape. "It might seem a bit daunting if this is your first security system, but you'll get used to it." He shoved a piece of paper in her face. "If you mess up, that's where you call. Give them your codes and they will call off the cavalry." A bell rang to indicate he was leaving.

"Wait!" she called out.

The man stopped in the doorway, turning to face her. His expression held his questions without the need for words.

"You are sure it is all working?" she asked, chomping on her bottom lip afterwards. "It isn't going to fizzle out the first time I try to use it, right?"

"Yeah," he said. "I tested it. That's my job. It's what I get paid to do. I have a lot of other calls to make today. Have a good one."

"Thanks," Bekka called out to her closing door.

The numbers on the paper were cringe worthy. Anything outside of her normal routine was. Creatures of habit weren't good with change. She'd been opening and closing the store since she was a young girl, in exactly the same way. Adding something new to the mix was as frightening as playing her music with someone listening. It simply didn't happen.

The palm of her hand hit her forehead. This wasn't a choice she could afford to make. The Velvet Violin was a robbery away from bankruptcy – the same as any other business on the block. She rounded the cash counter to twiddle her thumbs until the schools let out. The fact of the matter was; she didn't need to be there in the morning. No one came in until late afternoon, ever. That left plenty of time to worry about her first time closing up and opening again using the alarm. If she did it wrong, she'd have no one to blame but herself for ruining everything. She buried her face in her hands, letting out the breath of air she'd held a little too long.

"A cup of tea," Bekka declared, perking up. That was exactly what she needed to calm overactive nerves. At least that was what her mother always told her. There was no point to arguing with a dead woman over tradition. She headed to the back to put on the kettle.

Bekka glanced around the room, patiently waiting for the water to boil. It was a no-win situation. The longer she waited, the longer it took. If she left, however, the kettle would blow its whistle the moment her back was turned.

Her foot tapped on the ground, a hollow noise echoing back. She glanced down at the rug loosely covering the family treasure. As far back as she remembered it was always called it the vault, although it had no locks to speak of. Built by her grandfather, it was merely a hiding place that had remained a trusted family secret to that day. Inside was the one thing she couldn't allow to be stolen. According to a notebook of her ancestors, it was a lost relic of the music world: a violin dating back before the name Stradivarius was even thought of. Only a handful were made and even less surfaced. It was her pride and joy. One day, she'd find the nerve to play it. For now, it remained safely stashed away and only brought out for cleaning and maintenance.

Steam poured out of the kettle spout, its whistling noise making her jump back a step. One hand covered her chest as she caught her breath.

Hot water covered a ball-shaped silver holder, waiting patiently inside a white mug. There was nothing fresher than mixing one's own blend of tea leaves. Bekka blew on the liquid, hoping to cool it down enough for a sip. It was silly, really. It would be a few minutes before she could taste the brew. Any sooner and there'd be a burnt tongue to deal with. If that happened, it wouldn't only be the tea that had no flavour. Her taste buds would revolt for the rest of the day, making everything bland. Even worse were the tiny blisters that would form. The bubbles would drive her crazy for days, tongue rubbing against the back of her teeth trying to scratch them away.

The mug sat on the counter; the handle still steadfast in her grip. Bekka glanced to each side, before pulling out a paper from under the counter with her free hand. A mischievous smile crossed her lips. The tabloids were her guilty pleasure. It didn't matter if anything printed in them was real. If she wanted the truth she could turn on the television and watch the news.

Fantasy was what she craved as long as it was served with a side order of danger. Her knight, however, didn't have the shiniest of armour. In fact, it was more than a little tarnished. Still, he needed to ride in on his stallion and save the day – the from whom and why were technicalities that mattered very little. Heroes always wanted to save everyone and everything. That wasn't the plan in her dreams. When she closed her eyes and let her mind drift, she was the only one being saved. In the background, any number of classical pieces would be playing – there were a few that would set the atmosphere perfectly.

It wasn't as if her imagination was abnormal, other than the musical aspect. There were a lot of middle-aged women who toted around romance novels to whittle away at the doldrums of reality. In their minds, they played the leading lady swept off her feet by the muscular and super-sexy hero. He would be able to save the day and offer a dozen orgasms without lifting more than a finger. Bekka's choice for reading was no different, although probably a bit less erotic and a wee touch darker. She preferred a dash of action with an alien or demon or two thrown in for good measure in lieu of extra muscles, a motorcycle, and some tattoos. If she was going to fantasize, it was going to be a doozie – go big or go home. There was nothing to lose. It wasn't like any of it was ever going to come true.

Her free hand turned the pages, stopping at an unusual advertisement: Demons and followers seeking the key to the gates of hell and unusual artifacts. New cult members welcome. Apply at...

Her mouth dropped open. The address was less than two blocks from her shop and the meeting was on the one day of the week she took off. It was a sign. It had to be.

A chuckle escaped her lips. She never did anything outrageous in real life, but this was too good to be true. If it was only to take a quick peek, it couldn't hurt. Besides, she didn't have anything they were looking for. She didn't even have to go inside all the way. Showing up to a building was a whole lot easier than trying out for the symphony. Hopefully, it would be just as satisfying.

Chapter Three

Uriel's voice boomed louder than the one on the radio. There was no one to criticize him on a country back road. Cows didn't care if he sang off-key. The song ended, leaving him tapping his thumbs on the steering wheel in time to the tune now etched in his mind. He reached for the dial, turning it down a few notches.

The only thing missing was his horse. He would have traded a vehicle for Big Red any day. Technology had its advantages, but he missed the days when man and beast rode together as one.

With one arm rested on the open window, his truck sped down the winding asphalt. That was the only indication of civilization around, save for a few tractors, preparing the fields for planting. Uriel's nostrils flared, taking in the fresh country air.

That plan was executed better on paper, ending with a quick shake of his head and a twitching nose. It was fertilizing time on the farms. The fragrant scent of any animal's dung wasn't his favourite, although anything was better than the pollution and smog of the city. Unfortunately, that was exactly where he was heading.

He switched driving arms to reach into the glove compartment, his hand re-emerging with an unopened bottle of cheap cologne. According to the commercials, all the cowboys wore it. The seal broke under pressure from his thumb. A few drops landed on his finger, before the bottle was resealed and disappeared again.

His finger ran under his nostrils. They flared once again. This time, he was rewarded with a choking cough. *Phew.* The scent was stronger than a thousand gardenias. He held his arm out the window, letting the wind carry as much of the sickly perfume away as possible. He had a mind to write to the company. No cowboy in his right mind would wear such a scent.

The city crept up quickly, overtaking open fields and animals, and replacing them with buildings, pavement, and people. Each one was oblivious to the world around them. All that mattered was making it to their next appointment on time. It was a vicious cycle – wake up early – commute – work all day – commute – sleep. Making money was the only objective. Life was squeezed into the one or two days a week they had off – a depressing thought, even for a guy who could crack a joke about almost anything. Of course, that was Uriel's defence mechanism. Anytime something got under his skin, he made light of it. Hard times were easier to deal with that way. Anyone who had seen as many battles as he had, needed their own way of dealing with trauma.

He glanced over at his hat, covering a stack of tabloids. Each and every one had turned out to be a dud. It seemed almost impossible that not one had amounted to anything worth noting when it came to demonic activity. There had been a horse that could count, which turned into a fun outing – probably not possessed by the woman's deceased husband as she claimed, though.

Uriel sighed, letting out air and puffing out his cheeks. Honking and yelling meant he was almost at the downtown core. He rolled up his window, turning on the fan to circulate air. Normally, venturing that deep into what others referred to as civilization was a no-go for him. He didn't see anything civilized about how the people lived and acted when crammed into small spaces. Unfortunately, he needed new leads or he'd be heading home empty-handed. None of the others would have done that, not even Gabrielle and she hated spending time away from the house. He'd be tormented to no end. It was better to be the one making the jokes rather than ending up the butt of them.

Uriel's truck sputtered to a stop at the side of the road, garnering more than one disgruntle glance. It was out of place in a world that revolved around the shiny and new – he was out of place. The door creaked open, begging for a good lubrication. That would only prolong the inevitable by a day or two, though. Uriel already knew his trusty mechanical-steed was headed for greener pastures in the wrecking yard soon. It was on its last legs. The only thing stopping him from trading it in was value. Companies didn't make trucks to last anymore. It was all about forcing upgrades every few years, rather than longevity and value. The corporate world made a living off of squeezing every penny from their victims... patrons. It wasn't that he couldn't afford it. The horsemen had accumulated a more than satisfactory stockpile of wealth over the years to aid in their fight against demons. For Uriel, it was the principle of the matter.

He glanced back at his truck, considering whether or not he needed to lock it. No one was going to hop into a dying truck to steal it, though. If they did, they wouldn't get far. His pace quickened to a light jog, coming to a halt before a newspaper stand. He quickly gathered every noticeable tabloid and placed them on the small counter by a cash register.

"Is this all you have?" Uriel asked the owner of the stand.

The man eyed his patron up and down, nodding. "You looking for something in particular, sonny? Not that I don't appreciate the business, but I doubt you'll find any thing of value in them."

"Aliens," Uriel replied.

"Aliens?!" the man said, scrunching up his nose. He shook his head. "You hunting aliens? How do you plan on catching 'em if you find 'em?"

"Oh, I forgot gum," Uriel said, pulling out a clip of bills. He pulled a couple out of their holder and tossed them down on the papers.

"You gonna use gum to catch em?!" the man exclaimed.

Uriel chuckled. "No... to chew," he replied, waving off a plastic bag. "Those are bad for the environment."

He jogged back to his truck, the door greeting him with another squeak. He took his seat, tossing the old papers to the floor and replacing them with the new. It was hunting time! His thumb and finger pressed against the key, poised to turn the ignition.

Please answer the phone. Your brother is calling. Please answer the phone.

Uriel slouched back, his chest heaving up and down a few times, listening to the words recite before he swiped the screen to answer.

"What took you so long?" Michael complained. "It rang long enough."

"I was picking up some supplies," Uriel answered, not ready to admit he hadn't located any demon broods as of yet. He picked up the top tabloid and flipped it open, covering his steering wheel. "To what do I owe the honour of this call?"

"There's a new development we need to discuss," Michael explained. "We need you to return as soon as possible."

"I'm on a hot lead at the moment," Uriel lied. A lick of his fingertips helped to turn the page.

"What we have to discuss is as hot as the gates to hell opening up," Michael suggested. "We've found two keys."

Uriel's eye bulged, not from the words his brother uttered – he barely heard those – but from a full-page ad in the paper. He chuckled. "I need to stick around and check out one thing," he said. "I'll head back in a day or so." His thumb clicked end before his sibling had a chance to argue. With the phone turned off, he read over the advertisement again.

Demons and followers seeking the key to the gates of hell and unusual artifacts. New cult members welcome. Please apply in person on Monday the thirteenth. Any information provided will be duly rewarded.

An address was provided in the bottom right hand corner. All of the print was imposed over top of a picture of a church of some sort.

Uriel snorted a chuckle. At least whoever wrote the ad had a sense of humour. Monday technically was the worst day of the week. Pairing it with the thirteenth and superstition made it doubly frightening – much more so than if it fell on any other day, even Friday.

The whole thing was almost too good to be true. Either demons were becoming dumber or it was a hoax. He wasn't about to let it rest until he knew the truth – even if it meant hanging around the city for a little longer.

Chapter Four

Gabrielle flinched at every bash, bang, and heavy footstep coming from the hall. Those noises could only mean one thing; Michael was back and he wasn't happy. She'd grown used to her brother's temper over the years, but as of late, he'd been much more restrained. The new mellow Michael was a welcome improvement. Of course, it was Tara who deserved the credit for soothing the beast. The changes weren't restricted to him, either. Ryder had a similar effect on her as well. In a way, finding their mates had completed them – made them better, stronger. Perhaps the same would hold true for her other two brothers.

Michael grunted, making his presence in the room known.

"Did you talk to anyone?" Gabrielle asked, flipping through the pages of the same book for the hundredth time. She'd been over it and over it to no avail. Wherever the piece of parchment Ryder had found came from still wasn't clear.

Michael pulled out a chair from the table only to slam it back in again. "Raphael's not answering and Uriel blew me off. He said was investigating a lead then hung up. He must have turned his phone off, too."

"Did you tell him about Dante?" Gabrielle questioned, one eyebrow arched.

"I tried," Michael scoffed, his facing turning even more sour. Neither of his brothers ever listened to him. Sure he was a hothead, but that didn't mean his advice wasn't sound. "I don't know how much he heard." He ran his hands through his hair, exhaling sharply through flaring nostrils. "You should have made the call. They both answer to you."

"There were too many issues with that plan," Gabrielle answered. "Phones hate me. I doubt I would have gotten past dialing the first number. Did he mention where he was? Maybe you could take a drive out there and have a look-see."

"A look-see? I don't do that." Michael scoffed. "And he didn't tell me, anyway. I have no clue where either one of them are. We'll have to wait until they come back to fill them in."

"I don't like that plan," Gabrielle admitted.

"I don't either," Michael admitted. "There are only two keys left. I'm sure the demons are becoming a bit anxious. That makes them more dangerous."

"I'm sure their faith in Dante will be faltering, too. He will need to save face," Tara said, walking in on the conversation. "I don't need to be an expert in demonology to know that."

She planted a kiss on Michael's cheek. "There must be some clues as to where to go from here. We just need to find them."

"I've been over everything too many times to count," Gabrielle said. "If it's here, I can't find it." She sighed. "I feel helpless."

"We are helpless," Michael said. "It was set up that way. Each of us came upon our mates by chance. The same will happen with Uriel and Raphael, whether they like it or not."

"But why?" Gabrielle asked. "Why didn't Nakamire leave us information about all this? It doesn't make sense. What's the point to making us struggle to carry out his wishes?"

"Maybe it's a test?" Tara suggested, shrugging her shoulders. She took a seat at the long table, pulling a book closer to look at. The ancient language held no meaning for her.

"It feels more like a game," Michael snorted.

"I agree, and I think Dante's winning," Gabrielle said.

"We have rescued two keys," Michael blurted out, frustration etched in the form of frown lines on his face. "That puts us up two to zero. In my books that means we are ahead. It's simple math."

Gabrielle chuckled. "It's too easy. Dante let us win the first two rounds. I think he has something up his sleeve still. There is a method to his madness. I just haven't figured it out yet. He could have attacked Ryder and myself while we were vulnerable, but he chose not to. Until we have all four keys, I wouldn't consider us to be ahead."

"So what can we do?" Tara asked.

"Figure out what the parchment means," Gabrielle said. *"The key is only to be used when true love fails and one partner stands accused."*

"I think we need to find the rest of it to make heads or tails of the meaning," Michael complained. "We've been over those lines a million times. Where is Ryder, anyway?"

"He's out at the stables, taking a break," Gabrielle answered. "Let's grab some more books and look for hidden pockets. Maybe we'll get lucky and find something right under our noses. It only makes sense if the gods hid something it would be here in their home."

"You two ladies are much more suited to such things," Michael said. "I'm going to go see if I can jog anything loose from your boyfriend's mind."

"No hurting him," Gabrielle called out after her brother.

"No promises," Michael replied, waving one hand over his head as he strolled out the door.

"I'm sure he's kidding," Tara said.

I'm not," Gabrielle said. The two burst out into a round of tension breaking laughter.

"I'll start at one end," Tara suggested. "You take the other. We can meet in the middle."

"Sounds like a plan," Gabrielle agreed, tying her long white hair up so it was out of the way.

Chapter Five

Dante glanced down at the tabloid one more time. Stretching his neck from side to side, a loud crack echoed through the room at the same time the door opened.

"Come in," Dante ordered. "Don't stand there snivelling all day."

"You wanted to see me, sir?" Dean asked, his knees wobbling and lips trembling. "I came the moment I received the summons."

"Let me ask you a question," Dante began. "Do you believe our organization works well in the spotlight?"

"No, sir," Dean answered, his hand neatly tucked away behind his back. "Our activities fair best unseen by the public eye."

"Exactly!" Dante exclaimed. "So maybe you could explain this." He slammed the paper down on his desk. "Go on. Take a look."

Dean inched forward, his feet catching on uneven grooves in the stone flooring. He stumbled, stopping his descent on the desk with his hands, one palm on either side of the open tabloid. His eyes widened as he read the advertisement. "I-I..."

"Did you place this ad?" Dante bellowed.

"I did not, sir," Dean replied.

"You didn't?" Dante side-eyed the man standing before him. If nothing else the dribble of urine showing on the front of his pants meant he was too scared to lie. "If you had nothing to do with it, who did?"

Dean sighed. "I may have mentioned my new job to my girlfriend," he muttered. "She's a member of that particular chapter of the order."

Dante tossed his hands in the air, letting them smack down at his sides. "Your girlfriend," he scoffed. "You shared the details of a covert mission with a woman..." He paused long enough to fill a shot glass with alcohol and toss it back. Smacking his lips, he continued, "What would possess you to do such a thing?"

"I didn't think she'd act on it, sir," Dean admitted. "I was bouncing ideas off of her as to how to go about doing what you asked. It was to help me decide what to do, not to hand over the mission to her chapter. She must have misunderstood."

"Well, you got one thing right," Dante snarled. "You didn't think and neither did she. That leaves us with a mess to clean up. I do hope you haven't been dating long." His voice rose at the end of the sentence.

"A few months," Dean replied. "Why? Is there a rule about date within the organization? I wasn't aware of anything of the sort, if there was."

"No," Dante answered, his lips pursed into a frown. "There won't be any survivors when we are done, though. You do understand, don't you? They will all need to be eliminated for safety sake."

"All?!" Dean squeaked. He coughed away the surprise in his voice. "There are dozens of members in that particular branch. They are some of our most loyal..."

Dante held up his hands palm first. "We don't need any more imbeciles in our ranks. I assure you they won't be missed by us or anyone else." His eyebrows waggled. "Either I have your loyalty, or you can be the first casualty from this mess. You decide, but do it quickly. My patience is dwindling, as is my time for correcting the situation. We can't afford to lose another key."

"You have my loyalty," Dean blurted out. He coughed, straightening his collar. "I still feel a bit responsible, though. I am the reason they are all going to die."

"As you should," Dante barked back. "This is the price others pay for your loose tongue. Remember that next time you have the urge to bounce ideas off someone."

"Yes, sir," Dean responded, his heels clicking together in a formal stance.

"Good," Dante said. "I need you to gather a list of every music shop, conservatory, symphony, music teacher, and instrument repair shop in the city. Cross-reference it with family businesses that have existed for two or more generations. Eliminate anyone on the list who is married. Have that ready for when we leave in an hour."

"Am I going with you?" Dean questioned.

"Indeed," Dante answered. "You made the mess and you'll help clean it up. Or perhaps you would prefer to stay here and entertain one of my wives as your predecessor is doing?"

"No, sir," Dean replied. "I'll have the list and our bags packed by the top of the hour. Shall I make reservations?"

"No need," Dante said. "We are already expected."

Chapter Six

There was a full day before the published meeting time in the tabloid with nothing to do. The driver side bucket seat reclined. Uriel propped his legs up on the passenger seat dash, pulling his hat down over his face.

The sun was about to crest on the horizon and not even a squirrel was stirring. Keeping watch of the property all night hadn't been one of his better decisions. Areas less than two blocks away were alive with the hustle and bustle of everyday life – where he was sitting, however, was ominously quiet. It might as well have been a graveyard at midnight, with a full moon to boot.

He closed his eyes, allowing them the rest they so richly needed. It was the next best thing to sleep or a caffeine overdose. By allowing one of his senses to recuperate at a time, he could stay alert enough to catch any demons lurking in the shadows. Sight always came first. If he could see them, he could beat them. An unexpected yawn forced a quick inhale.

The undeniable scent of honeysuckle drifted past his nostrils, eagerly awaking them and tickling the tip of a memory that wouldn't quite form. Uriel tipped the cowboy hat up off his face enough to take a peek from whence the subtle scent came.

Long red hair. It wasn't the same as his own, which was much lighter. It was a more robust auburn shade that warmed him from the inside, in the same manner as a shot of similar coloured spirits drunk on a cold day might. A light breeze blew a few strands toward him. He inhaled deeply, allowing the sweet fragrance to remind him how long it had been since a woman had stolen his attention. The urge to gaze upon more than just her back took over.

"Excuse me, ma'am, are you lost?" he asked.

Bekka jumped back two steps. "No," she blurted out, a frown etched onto her otherwise flawless skin. "Why would you think that?"

"You are standing in the middle of a street," Uriel replied, adding a signature wink onto the end of the comment. "And, I might add, staring at a church dedicated to demon worship. Are you a member of their ranks?"

"No," Bekka replied, shaking her head. "I-I was just curious. I thought I'd check it out and see what all the fuss is about."

"Well, ma'am," he tipped his hat back to its proper position, "I hope you won't take this the wrong way, but I don't think this is a proper place for a pretty lady like yourself to be lurking about. Demons and their followers can be a bit rough. I wouldn't want you to get hurt."

Heat rushed to Bekka's cheeks. The reason for her blush wasn't as cut and dried as being a smidge embarrassed, although that was a part of the problem. "I think I can decide for myself where I want to be or don't want to be, thank you," she blurted out. "I don't need some stuck in the past cowboy impersonator to tell me, either." Her arms crossed over her chest in a huff. The red colouring in her cheeks began to spread, taking over her entire face.

"Perhaps you should at least move to the sidewalk," Uriel suggested. "It's about time for morning rush hour. The middle of the road might not be a good place to stand."

"Why don't you move to the sidewalk?" She stomped off. There'd be an entire day to sulk over the stupidity of that reply in the peace and quite of her own store.

Uriel chuckled, watching her skulk down the street a few blocks, before disappearing into a shop, although from where he sat, he couldn't see exactly which one. If he wasn't on a mission, he might have followed. As it was, though, he had his hands full. The circus was coming to town and he had front row tickets.

Chapter Seven

Bekka let the door slam behind her, something she rarely did. A little too much pressure would mean the need to replace the aging entrance. She plopped down on her stool, letting her forehead bang against the counter a few times.

"Hey." Veronica's voice melded with the chimes on the door. She was a singer through and through. She inhaled deeply. "Did you buy the same perfume as me?"

"We're not open yet," Bekka replied, looking up only long enough to confirm the person was, in fact, her one and only friend before banging her head back down again. "And you don't own the corner market on scents. I happen to like the way this one smells."

The two girls not only grew up together, but also in their younger years, could have passed for twins, sporting the same deep auburn coloured hair and brown eyes with golden specks. Their mothers played dress up with them, buying them the same outfits and making sure the two had matching haircuts. It wasn't until puberty hit that things changed.

Veronica blossomed in body and spirit, while Bekka remained the same. Bekka's parents always said their friendship was destiny, and for all intents and purposes, they remained as close as any two sisters could be – squabbles and all.

"Whoa!" Veronica exclaimed. "What's got you down?" She took the liberty of flipping the sign on the door to open.

"I did it again," Bekka answered. Her bottom lip jutted out in a pathetic pout. "I shouldn't be allowed in public. It isn't safe." Jealousy was an ugly emotion – one she wasn't about to admit to feeling. If it had been Veronica who met the cowboy that morning, she'd be at a rodeo by now.

Veronica chuckled, taking the second stool behind the counter for herself. "What did you do this time? I hope you didn't yell at some innocent old lady." A piece of gum twirled between two fingers, stretching to a thin strand from plump lips. She gobbled it back up again.

"No," Bekka whined. "It's worse. It was a guy."

"A guy!" Veronica screeched. "What guy?"

"I don't know him," Bekka snapped back. Mentioning a male prospect in front of her friend was a mistake. There had never been a friends first rule in Veronica's book. "I doubt I'll ever see him again. I was quite rude. I don't know why I blurt things out before thinking about them." She bit her bottom lip, leaving a small indent. He had called her pretty. This was why she never dated – her big mouth always got in the way. The worst part was, this guy was cute. There was no escaping what had already been done, though. Life rules stated: there was never a second chance to make a first impression.

"Speaking of guys..."

"Oh, no," Bekka said. "Not today. I'm not going to lunch or dinner to sit at a table alone in case you need a way out. I swear, you need to learn to swipe the other way a few times!"

"I wish I could explain it," Veronica said. "It's a feeling that someone is out there waiting for me. I know it sounds weird, but I have to find him. Besides, you don't have to go anywhere."

"Thank goodness," Bekka replied in a huff. "I'm not in the mood for watching you date after ruining a chance of my own."

"He's meeting me here," Veronica blurted out.

"What?!" Bekka exclaimed. "Why would you have him come here?"

"He is interested in music," Veronica said. "He wanted to see me play, but I don't know him from a hole in the ground. I wasn't about to invite him to my place. That wouldn't be safe."

"So you invited him to mine?!" Bekka screeched. "How is that safe for me?"

"Oh, relax," Veronica suggested, applying her fifth coat of red lipstick. "It's not like you live here, or anything."

"No," Bekka agreed. "I do, however, work long hours and close up after dark. If I end up dead or missing, it's on your shoulders."

"You are assuming this guy is horrid," Veronica complained. "He could very well be the one. We do both love music and Italian food."

"Then you should have had a spaghetti picnic in the park," Bekka snapped. "You could have taken turns serenading each other."

The door chimes sounded. Both girls glanced over at a thin man wearing a black suit. He pulled his sunglasses off, giving both women a once over before heading to the back of the store.

"Do you think that's him?" Bekka whispered. "I don't usually have customers this early."

"I don't know," Veronica admitted. "In the picture the guy was younger and I didn't notice a bald spot. Here..." She loaded up her dating app. "What do you think?"

Bekka shrugged her shoulders. There were similarities between the man and the profile picture. They could have been father and son.

"What should I do?" Veronica asked.

The man glanced over his shoulder at them. "Change the subject," Bekka whispered back.

"Tell me about the guy you met," Veronica said, articulating loud and clear.

Bekka slapped her forehead. That wasn't the topic she had hoped for. "I told you I messed up," she replied through gritted teeth.

"Tell me more," Veronica prodded. "Where were you?"

"I was down the street," Bekka answered, pulling out the tabloid. She pointed to the ad. "I read this the other day, and I thought it was interesting. I was checking things out."

"Demon worship?!" Veronica exclaimed. "What in the world possessed you to check that out?"

"It's not that big a deal," Bekka said, rolling her eyes. "I was curious. Anyway, he was lying back in his truck, parked across the street from the place. I didn't see him there and happened to be standing in front of the driver's side window, having a look-see. That's when he said hi."

"Hi?" Veronica said, one eyebrow arched. "You yelled at him for saying hi? That's a new low, for even you."

"No," Bekka blurted out. "It startled me, though. That threw me off my game. Then he suggested I might not be safe there."

"I'm sorry," the man said, interrupting. "I couldn't help but overhear your conversation. Allow me to introduce myself: I'm Aaron. You must be my date?" He bowed.

"Yes," Veronica giggled. "I'm sorry I didn't recognize you."

"No worries there," Aaron said. "This stranger you speak of has me a bit concerned, though. What did he look like?"

"A cowboy," Bekka replied, shrugging her shoulders. "From what I could tell, he was in his late twenties."

"You can do a bit better than that," Veronica complained. "That doesn't even qualify as a description. It's only an age range."

"Fine," Bekka huffed. "He was attractive, muscular, and sexy. Is that better?"

"I don't think I could figure out who he was from that," Aaron chuckled. "Perhaps a few more details might help."

"He had red hair," Bekka started, her eyes closing, "not like mine, but lighter. His eyes were a shade of green that I thought was reserved specifically for the colour of the ocean in tropical ads – the ones selling trips to the perfect getaway resort. Under the sleeves of his T-shirt, muscles rippled as if they were complaining about being restrained by the fabric. Strength, power, and electricity flowed through him. I can still feel the tingling sensation his mere words caused. It was exhilarating and frightening at the same time – as if he wasn't a normal person, but rather supernatural in some way – like a vampire or werewolf, if you know what I mean."

"Okay," Veronica blurted out, stopping the fantasy before it became a little too detailed for mixed company. "He's a dreamboat, from a fantasy land." She fanned herself with a flyer. "Men like that don't come around often."

"That's very helpful," Aaron said, changing the direction of the conversation. "You said he was driving a truck, right?"

"Yes," Bekka agreed. "Why?"

"I am the head of the order that owns the building in question," Aaron admitted. "We'll make sure he moves along and doesn't cause anyone else any problems."

"You're a devil worshipper?" Veronica asked, adding a nervous chuckle onto the end. "How interesting. That wasn't mentioned on your profile."

"You stated religion wasn't an important issue," Aaron replied. "Technically, it's demonology. I don't have any affiliation with what this world calls the devil or Satan. We have a different belief system. I think you'll find the two are actually incomparable. Of course, if it bothers you, we can call our date off right now. I was hoping to hear you play, though. Music is one passion we all can equally enjoy. It has no prejudice; nor does it hold grudges. Your profile said you give lessons to children. Which instrument do you specialize in?"

"I play several," Veronica admitted. "Most of the classes are for the violin and recorder. My true passion lies in the piano, though."

"Ah, the piano," Aaron repeated. "And what about you, Miss? Do you play any instruments?"

"Me?!" Bekka shrieked, her face turning red. "I-I."

"She plays the violin," Veronica announced. "She's brilliant, too."

"Fascinating," Aaron cooed. "I'd be honoured to hear your music as well. Do you have a specific violin you prefer to play?"

"I don't play in front of people," Bekka blurted out, her breathing becoming erratic and heart rate escalating.

Veronica alternated glances between the two. "Perhaps we should grab a coffee?" she suggested. "There's a lovely little café down the street a few blocks."

"Sounds wonderful," Aaron agreed, his gaze still fixed on Bekka. "It was a pleasure meeting you..." He paused. "I'm afraid I didn't catch your name."

"That's because I didn't tell you it," Bekka snapped.

"I can see why you alienated the other young man," Aaron said, chuckling. "Sometimes in life, people are simply being nice. Not everyone means to offend. Shall we?" He extended his arm.

Veronica latched on. "It's probably a good idea." She glanced back, mouthing the word sorry. The door chimed as they exited.

Bekka slammed her head on the counter. She'd done it again. Twice in one day she alienated someone for simply speaking to her. Dealing with people was something she was never meant to do. There was only one thing that could rectify the situation: head to the back and put on a pot of tea. That was her one solution for everything. She paused, glancing down at the hidden compartment beneath her feet. She'd been playing the violin for all her life. There was no reason to fear others hearing her music. If only she had Veronica's confidence...

She planted her feet firmly, forming her favourite superhero pose. Determination was her power. The next man she met she was going to be nice to, even if it killed her.

Chapter Eight

"Slow down," Dante ordered, knocking on the glass partition between the backseat and the driver. Flying was one form of transportation he'd never become used to. There were too many variables involved for his liking, and enough problems on the roads, without worrying about the skies as well.

The limousine driver nodded, obeying the command. The car slowed to a crawl in front of the old church, its lawn littered with the worst society had to offer. The area was a scene from before a big event, with tents pitched, barbecues smoking, and a variety of different rock songs blaring.

Dante glanced out the window at the lines gathering in front of the largest chapter of demonology in the district. "Look at them all. You can tell from the empty look on their faces how useless each and every one of them is. This much attention is sure to bring out the local authorities, too. Let's hope it doesn't reach any further than that."

"It won't be easy to murder the entire order," Dean suggested. "We could be caught. Maybe we should forget about it."

"Nice try," Dante snickered. "We are going to use the publicity to our advantage. Look... over there." He pointed at a group of plump women wearing floral dresses toting signs of hate. That was religion at its finest. Destroy all who don't believe. Not one of them thought, perhaps, it was their beliefs that were wrong or questioned their actions. They blindly followed what they were told was true. "The kingdom of God is among us! Rejoice!" He let out a hearty laugh. "They will be our salvation."

"I'm not sure I understand, sir," Dean admitted.

"The good are always quick to exact punishment," Dante explained. "Wars have been fought over religion for centuries. It isn't a far stretch that a group of extremists would take justice into their own hands in this situation."

"You're going to make them scapegoats!" Dean exclaimed.

"I might not have to," Dante replied. "They might just take care of things for us. If not, they won't mind taking the credit or calling it the will of their Lord. A just and righteous god who kills." His laughter trailed off into a serious stare. "The list." He held out his hand.

"Here," Dean replied, holding out a piece of paper. "I put in all of the variables you asked for. There aren't a lot of names left."

"Splendid," Dante replied, a grin returning. "We'll use the scientific approach." He closed his eyes, paper in one hand. With his other, he motioned with one finger in a circle several times before allowing it to land on the page. "The Velvet Violin is our winner. Have the driver take us there. It doesn't appear to be too far. Perhaps we can end our search early."

"What is it we are looking for?" Dean asked.

"That is exactly your problem," Dante replied. "You don't have a clue what is going on. If you, or your so-called girlfriend, had read any of the materials on the current project, you would know." He shook his head. "We are looking for a specific instrument that predates known violins and a very specific violinist – their music would be that which legends are built on."

"Why would they be in a small shop?" Dean questioned. "If they are that talented, shouldn't they be famous and playing in an orchestra somewhere?"

Dante backhanded his assistant across the face. "Fool!" he yelled. "I had hoped you still had promise, but perhaps your fate will be no different than your girlfriend's will be."

"I apologize, sir," Dean stuttered. "I should have known better than to question your methods. I beg for another chance."

"It's the ninth inning, two outs and you are at bat with two strikes against you," Dante stated. "The next pitch is either a home run or you're out."

"Understood, sir," Dean said, wiping the sweat from his brow. He knocked on the glass partition, nodding at the driver. "The Velvet Violin."

The driver acknowledged the request. His foot pressing down on the petal, the church and its new-found fame became but a blur left behind.

Chapter Nine

Uriel chuckled to himself. Not even he had been prepared for the number of people who were responding to the ad. Apparently, this city was filled with wannabe demon worshippers. He leaned back, keeping a watchful eye on the doors to the old church. They hadn't opened as of yet, but were bound to at any time. If they didn't, there was going to be a riot.

His hat kept his face hidden, in case there was anyone who might have recognized him. Demons were well aware of the individual appearances of the four horsemen. Their images had most likely been circulated through the majority of the chapters, siphoning down through their followers. As long as his line of sight remained unobstructed, he'd catch all the details of the day.

As if on cue, a stretch limousine slowed, blocking his sight. Apparently, the advertisement had attracted some well-to-do attention, as well as the usual scum he associated with demons and their followers. Tinted windows shielded the passengers, if there were any, from identification. The limo crawled at a snail's pace, before speeding up again. Brake lights flashed a couple of blocks up, almost exactly where the woman had disappeared earlier. A coincidence...

"Hey," an officer yelled, tapping on the truck's window with a flashlight. "What are you doing in there?"

The last thing Uriel wanted was to tango with the local law enforcement, especially without a long stem rose to clench between his teeth. In the end it would only serve to make his job a million times more difficult. The window rolled down. "I parked to find my bearings," he lied, holding up a map. "My phone died and I was looking for a place to grab a coffee and recharge."

"What's wrong with your truck? Can't you recharge in there?" The officer questioned.

"It's an older model," Uriel replied. "I even have to wind the windows by hand. There's no power anything in this baby."

"Maybe you should get a new truck," the officer joked, chuckling to himself. "We had a report of a stranger lurking around these parts."

Uriel glanced at the officer and then behind him. "And you came to me first. I'm honoured." He rubbed his face, pulling on the corners of his mouth to erase the smile trying to form. "There's a whole lawn of suspicious folks right behind you."

The officer glanced over his shoulder then back again. "Are you trying to get smart with me?" he asked. "Don't try to tell me how to do my job, son. I've been policing these here streets longer than you've been alive."

"I doubt that," Uriel whispered under his breath.

"What was that?" the officer asked.

"I was just wondering if you could recommend a coffee shop nearby," Uriel lied, allowing a smile to grace his lips in a friendly manner.

"Up the street there are plenty," the officer replied. "Get your coffee and phone charge, but I don't want to hear any more complaints about you loitering in this area. Now, skedaddle. I don't want to see this truck of yours parked anywhere near that there church again." He slapped the side of the truck twice, as if it were a horse he wanted to move out.

The words *any more complaints* meant his identity had been made by someone. The question was, by who? The engine roared with the turn of the key. The officer was already preoccupied in his car with a coffee and a box of donuts. Uriel kept the man and the church in view from the rear mirror as he moved up a block, heading down a side street to find the cover of a few buildings. A U-turn brought him back into range again. All he needed to do was find a coffee and pretend he was just finishing up if he had a run-in with the law again.

Having to move didn't bother him nearly as much as who had reported him for loitering. No one had come out of the building and he had kept a low profile. The only people who might have seen him were in the limousine that passed by.

He slapped his forehead. There had been the woman. If she were a member of the order, she wouldn't have hesitated to report him for hanging about, especially after he called the worship dangerous. From his new vantage point; he had no view of the spot where she disappeared. Intuition insisted she was involved somehow, and if that was true, she had the edge on him.

Uriel shook his head. He needed to stick to his guns. He was there to eliminate demons and make sure none of the keys surfaced. Wherever the woman fit in, didn't matter in the end. She was out of sight, now he needed her out of mind.

Chapter Ten

Bekka sat with her face down, nose buried between the pages of the latest tabloid. The steam from the ceramic mug in one hand rose up, threatening to reach the smoke alarms. It wouldn't have been the first time something silly like that had happened to her. The system was far too sensitive. It was door chimes that sounded instead, though.

"Back so soon?" Bekka snickered without looking up. "That was the fastest date in history. What happened?"

"I didn't realize I was on a date," Dante replied, arching one eyebrow.

"I-I'm sorry,' Bekka stuttered. "I thought you were someone else." She bit her lip, remembering her vow. "How can I help you?"

"Are you the owner of this delightful shop?" Dante asked.

"Yes, but I'm not looking to sell." Bekka cringed at the words. She'd gone and done it again, alienating someone with her first few words. Her posture tensed, easing again at the sound of warm laughter.

"I wasn't looking to buy the whole place," Dante said. "I'm a curator of fine instruments. It's been a passion of mine since I was a wee lad." He flashed a smile, showing off a set of perfect teeth. "It turned into a professional hobby. I acquire instruments for various orchestras across the country. Do you play?"

"A little," Bekka replied, her cheeks pink.

"I think you might be selling yourself short," Dante said. He removed a violin from its case and handed it to her, along with a sheet of music. "Would you mind? I need to hear the instrument to know if it will be a good fit for what I am looking for."

Bekka licked her lips. As much as playing for an audience frightened her, she needed the sale. The sheet music shook in her hand. "This is my favourite piece! How did you know?"

"I didn't," Dante admitted. "It seems we have something in common, as it is also one of my favourites. There is nothing better than the classics. Today's music is lost noise in comparison."

A smile formed on Bekka's lips as she gave the stranger a once over. He wasn't like the other two men she met earlier. The cowboy was rough and the twang of country music could have easily gotten on her nerves. Not that she cared if he listened to it. Live and let live. Some form of music was better than none at all. Aaron was, for lack of a better description, trying too hard. The man before her was a man among men -

a true gentleman. If she landed him, it would be Veronica's turn to be jealous. It was time to throw caution to the wind.

A music stand took over the job of holding the sheet. Rosin rubbed up and down the hairs of the bow, preparing it for the task at hand. Bekka took her stance, straightening her posture. A deep breath of air helped relax the tension from her hands and fingers. She'd gone through those motions thousands of times and knew exactly what needed to be done. Playing the violin only appeared easy to onlookers. The truth was, it took years of practice for most people to learn even the simplest of tunes. Of course, Veronica was the exception to every rule. She had a natural affinity for music. Bekka's anxiety levels began to rise. Pent-up emotions were the worst thing for any performer. She went over the procedures in her head, one more time, erasing all other thoughts.

The key was all in the grip. Complete control of the bow was essential. Losing it would produce unappealing squeaks rather than the rich tones seasoned violinists created. She closed her eyes, envisioning herself in a rowboat on a lake. Her fingers gently skimmed across the water, sending out perfect ripples. Her bow became the fingertips, the strings – the lake's surface; the ripples – the sweet sounds of her music filling the room.

Dante applauded the final notes. "That was simply perfection," he praised. "My dear, you should be playing in the finest orchestras."

Bekka's smile doubled in size. "It's been a dream of mine," she admitted. "I haven't had the nerve to audition, though."

"You must," Dante said. "I hope this isn't a bit forward, but the conservatory is having a gala tomorrow night. Perhaps you should be there."

"I know," Bekka replied. "It is for the best musicians in the country." She heaved out a heavy breath. "I'm afraid I am not on that list."

"You are now," Dante said, grinning. "If you would do me the honour of accompanying me, I promise it will be a night to remember."

Bekka's jaw dropped. "Yes!" she exclaimed. "I'd be honoured."

"Excellent," Dante beamed. "This could lead to auditions. Most musicians have a particular instrument they play for such events. Do you have one, or should we try out a few from your selection, just in case?"

"No," Bekka gushed. "I mean yes. I have one I can play if asked to audition. I keep it safely hidden away so it doesn't get damaged."

"As it should be," Dante said. "I'll pick up at about eight tomorrow night, then." He headed toward the door.

"Wait," Bekka called out. "What should I wear?"

Dante chuckled. "Leave that to me." The chimes on the door rang and he was gone. Only the mixed scents of cigar and whisky remained as proof he existed at all.

Bekka inhaled deeply, savouring his fragrances. Excitement bubbled, overflowing in the form of an impromptu dance. She was going on a date and it was ten times better than anything Veronica experienced in the last year. She hadn't needed a dating app to find him, either.

Chapter Eleven

Veronica tugged on the door. It should have opened easily, but it was locked. The open sign faced forward, mocking her additional attempts. One hand became a shield as she peered through the window, the sun beating down on her back.

It wasn't like her friend to close up midway through the afternoon. A lot of things weren't like the Bekka she knew as of late – from snarky comments, to the way she treated strangers. Her friend's attitude was changing and it wasn't necessarily for the better. That was the reason Veronica put her date on hold. Under normal circumstances, the coffee would have lasted long enough that she could officially send a message suggesting they pursue other opportunities in the dating world. She already knew Aaron wasn't the one. Still, she agreed to meet up later just to come back and check in at the music store. Bekka was more than a best friend. She was family – a sister. They even shared the same birthdate. How their parents had managed that was beyond her. It must have taken some fancy planning.

Veronica moved to a position that had less of a glare. Another red flag flew into the air. Bekka was dancing around the room. The palm of her hand banged on the glass. With no response, she formed a fist and rapped as loudly as possible. The whole pane vibrated, but it did the trick. She had her friend's attention.

"What on earth are you doing?!" Bekka shrieked.

"I was going to ask you the same thing," Veronica said. "I've never seen you lock up in the afternoon before." She paused, frowning. "I've also never seen you dance around a room. You used to make fun of me for doing that."

"Why are you here? Did your date crap out?" Bekka snapped.

"Not exactly," Bekka admitted. "I was worried you were down in the dumps. I told Aaron I'd see him tonight. Are you okay?"

"I'm better than okay," Bekka said, spinning in a circle. A display of replacement rosin crashed to the ground.

"Be careful!" Veronica shrieked.

"It's fine," Bekka replied, flicking her wrist at the mess. "I'll clean it up later."

Veronica grabbed her arm, pulling her closer. She glanced at each eye. "Are you taking drugs? If you are, you can tell me. There are places that can help."

Bekka pulled away. "I'm not taking drugs!" she exclaimed. "Can't I be happy for a change, or is that emotion reserved only for you?"

"What?!" Veronica cried out. "I want you to be happy. I am concerned at how fast your moods are swinging, though, not to mention the highs and lows. Maybe you should see a doctor."

"Don't be silly," Bekka replied. "You don't need to worry anymore and you didn't have to end your date. I am more than fine. I have a date of my own."

"That's amazing!" Veronica exclaimed, taking her friend's hand in her own. "Tell me all about it. Is it the cowboy? Did he come looking for you?"

Bekka ripped herself away once again. "No," she said, her shoulders swaying. "It wasn't the cowboy. He wasn't the one, anyway. I see that now. I need a softer touch... a gentleman's hand. That's exactly what I found, too."

"When? Where?" Veronica asked.

"Here," Bekka replied. "He acquires instruments for orchestras and famous musicians. After showing some interest in one of my violins, he requested I play it for him... to test the sound. So I did."

Veronica's jaw dropped. "You played in front of him? That's amazing. This could open so many doors for you. This time next year, I'll be able to say I know someone famous. Where is he taking you?"

"The conservatory is having a gala tomorrow night," Bekka said, pretending to check the polish on her nails. It was a meaningless exercise. She hadn't had a manicure in her life, nor did she paint them. "He thought I deserved to be there."

"This is so exciting!" Veronica shrieked. "Have you thought about what you are going to wear?"

"Actually," Bekka started, chimes interrupting her.

"I have a package for the owner," the courier announced.

"Here," Bekka announced, holding out her hand to take the handheld device, requiring acknowledgement. She scribbled her name. Her signature never looked the same on the screen as it did on paper, but the person delivering packages seldom seemed to mind.

A pair of scissors made short work of the packing tape. The box was open before the chimes from the courier's exit finished ringing. Bekka pulled out a beautiful full-length dress. The all-black bodice flared out into a skirt. Frills faded through multiple shades, beginning with black transitioning through greys and ending with white.

"This," Bekka said, her eyes twinkling a smile. "This is what I am going to wear. It's perfect, don't you think?"

"It's beautiful," Veronica said. "Where'd you get it? It looks like an original design. It must have cost a fortune."

"My date sent it for me," Bekka admitted. "He didn't want me to have to worry about whether my outfit was appropriate for the gala."

"He has exquisite taste," Veronica said. "What's his name?"

Bekka placed the dress on the counter. "Huh," she huffed. "I don't know. I never asked him." She giggled.

Veronica grabbed the box. "There's no return name or card," she mumbled, a frown creasing her otherwise perfect complexion.

"I guess I'll find out tomorrow night," Bekka said, shrugging her shoulders. "It's a small detail."

"Promise me you'll be careful," Veronica said. "Knowing a man's name isn't a tiny detail. This doesn't feel right."

"Says the girl who goes out with anyone who shows even an ounce of interest on a phone app," Bekka scoffed. "At least I know what he looks like. You couldn't even tell if Aaron was your date or not."

"He also didn't buy me an expensive dress without dropping his name," Veronica argued. "I just don't want you to get hurt."

"Or perhaps you just want to keep every guy for yourself," Bekka hissed. "I think you should go. Don't come back until you are ready to support me the way I have you for years."

"Bekka!" Veronica shrieked.

"Go." Bekka pointed at the door. "Before you ruin my mood."

Veronica glanced back at the shop. The hairs on the back of her neck stood at attention – even they knew something was wrong. There wasn't anything that could be done about it, though. Bekka was a big girl. Hopefully, she had the wherewithal to know if this mystery man was a creep in disguise. With her friend's lack of experience in dating, however, it didn't seem likely.

Chapter Twelve

Uriel stretched, a yawn tagging along for the ride. Sitting in any vehicle, waiting for something to happen wasn't exciting work. Every time he was forced to endure a long bout of surveillance, he understood a little more the local law enforcement's preoccupation with donuts and coffee. A few sprinkles broke up the monotony that came part and parcel with a stakeout.

He rubbed the back of his neck and prepared to watch the sun set for yet another day. Mortals had no idea how lucky they were to make it through a full rotation of the planet. The odds were stacked against them to start with. Their haphazardly approach to the gift they'd been given made things even worse. His eyes focused on the horizon, hoping to see it set a fire in a blaze of glory. A red sky at night was one of the oldest predictions of good fortune for any battle to come. Alas, the light simply faded away to darkness.

The crowd, whether pro-demon-worship or against it, began clearing out shortly after lunch. It appeared as if nothing happened. The advertisement had been an elaborate hoax, a bank robbery across town garnering the blame. The large crowd attracted law enforcement officers, and kept them at bay, while the theft took place. The financial institution wasn't the only place hit, either. Thieves targeted a series of smaller stores and gas stations as well. Uriel chuckled. These criminals actually had made out like bandits.

Uriel yawned a second time. As much as he loved the outdoors, stargazing simply wasn't his thing. That activity was reserved for his brother, Raphael. There wasn't a celestial formation his sibling didn't know the name and meaning of – the first true astronomer.

A shrill scream grabbed his attention. Uriel's eyes narrowed, squinting in the direction of the building under surveillance. It was hard to make out, but there were two figures. If the physical yells weren't enough, their body language signalled they were fighting. That was his cue. Even if it wasn't demon related, at least his legs could stretch for a bit. A minute ago he'd been just about ready to throw in the towel anyway. This gave him a story he could up sell back home.

Uriel hopped out of his truck, taking the most direct route toward the commotion. The closer he came, the worse he found the unfolding circumstances to be.

"Tsk-tsk," Uriel gasped. "Women don't like being forced to bend to a man's rule." He tipped his hat back, gauging reaction to his words.

"I don't know who you are mister, but you best be moving along," the man said, his grip tightening around the woman's wrist. "This is none of your concern. You'd be best off keeping it that way."

The woman winced, pain radiating in her whimpers. Uriel took a step forward. "Why don't you let her go and we'll settle this between us?" he suggested.

The wind howled with excitement, alerting all of nature to an upcoming battle over a young maiden in distress. Uriel inhaled. The sweet fragrance of honeysuckle stole his attention. He'd smelt it there before. He turned for a better glimpse of the woman. She looked similar to the one he'd spoken to, but he couldn't be sure in the lighting – or more specifically the lack thereof.

It might have only been a split second, but he'd lost his focus nonetheless and it cost him. A fist landed square on his jaw, followed by a dagger to his side. His cowboy hat floated down to the ground in slow motion. He'd managed to step out of the way of a death blow, but only by a smidge. Fingers covered in blood reached for his belt, unlatching a rope. He twirled it in a circle.

"Ma'am, you better run," he suggested, his eyes not willing to leave his target again. He couldn't be sure she listened to his advice. If she was the same woman he'd met earlier, she probably had a problem with him giving her orders. This set was for her own safety, though. If she couldn't see that, she'd run the risk of becoming collateral damage. That was on her.

The man spewed swear words violently at the sight of Uriel's weapon, running for the building. The chase was on.

Whatever lurked within the building was about to be uncovered. The door opened, a spotlight shining down on the man's balding head. Beads of sweat flew from his face as he zipped through the entrance, screaming.

Uriel chuckled. "Nice of you to round 'em up for me," he snickered, heading up the stairs. He felt his side, blood still slowly trickling from the wound. A scratch that size wasn't about to keep him from answers, though. He tossed the front doors open, unhinging one in the process.

The interior looked and smelt as any number of religious institutions he'd come across in the past, save for one thing; a complete lack of artifacts. There were no stained-glass windows, paintings, or crosses. Uriel ran a single finger along the top of a pew. His lips puckered, blowing a thick layer of dust from the tip. The main room wasn't used for worship purposes. He'd seen it before. These groups preferred basements and cellars for their activities, especially if there were secret passages involved.

Uriel continued his stroll up the main aisle toward the altar. Nine out of ten times, demon followers used religious shrines to cover up where the real ceremonies took place. It also made a great hiding place.

"Come out, come out, wherever you are," Uriel hummed, wondering if perhaps the man had recognized his face. That was one of the main reasons he wore the hat – well that and it looked cool. One hand pushed everything on the altar, hoping a candlestick or tarnished chalice might be what opened the staircase leading down. Nothing happened. He replaced the rope on his belt, needing both hands. Placing his palms against stone, he pushed with all his might. The fixture refused to budge.

Uriel sighed, taking a few steps backward. His foot caught on a loose piece of carpet. He glanced down. This bunch was lazier than he anticipated. The carpet came up easily, revealing a trapdoor, which wasn't even hidden. The latch squeaked a warning to those below as it prepared for it's final opening.

Uriel glanced at the ladder leading down. It wasn't the ideal set-up. On a descent, he'd be a sitting duck begging for an ambush. Demons were rarely smart enough to figure out such a plan, but men always had such potential.

He took in a deep breath, acknowledging that he'd come too far to walk away now. No horseman even showed fear of an upcoming battle. Fights like this were what they lived for.

One hand on each rail, Uriel bypassed the steps, sliding to the bottom. The skin on his palms wore thin, but slivers were the least of his concerns. He spun around to nothing but a set of torches lighting a corridor. He was being summoned to a party and it would be rude to refuse. All cowboys were gentlemen, first and foremost, in their own way.

Flames flickered among whispers, threatening to extinguish. Darkness held no sway over Uriel, though. He welcomed fights fought at a disadvantage. Years of training his senses to deal with the lack of one or another gave him the upper hand in such battles. The torches could continue mocking him. It mattered not – he would have the last laugh if they followed through with their threats.

The church upstairs and down might have been a relic of the past, but the doors at the end of the hallway were not. They swung open as Uriel approached, beckoning him to enter. With such a fancy greeting, there was no way he could refuse. He inched inside, his lips twitching at the corners. A smile formed as he faced a room of adversaries at the ready.

"I'll give you all a fighting chance," Uriel said, chuckling. He reached for his lasso once again, twirling it high above his head.

"A rope," the man cackled. "You plan to take down all of us with a rope? We are twenty-four to your one. You can't win."

"I rather like those odds," Uriel replied, letting loose on his grip. His palm faced down toward the rope without touching it as it flew toward its target. It curled over a group of men. Once latched, he reached out grabbing the slack and pulling it into his hip.

"And now what?" the man said, yelling over the voices of the three men grunting and groaning their displeasure. "You have them caught and we are all still free. That leaves you without a weapon."

"This," Uriel answered, pulling the rope tight. It's threads turned to blades, slicing the men in half where they stood.

"Get him," the man ordered.

A group of men approached from all sides. Uriel's hand remained steadfast on his rope, his knees bent, ready for action.

"Draw your weapons," the man yelled, continuing to bark orders in the background.

The others complied, unsheathing swords and daggers. Reflections of flames flickered in the shiny metal of the blades.

"You brought a rope to a sword fight," the man mused. "That was a fatal mistake. Only a fool would enter a fight with such a weapon."

Uriel dropped his rope. "No arguments there," he agreed. Two guns appeared in his hand. A series of quick fire shots went off; leaving the men in piles on the ground, blood trickling from their wounds. "You brought knives to a gunfight. Who looks foolish now?" he chuckled.

The remaining three turned to flee. Uriel tossed a shiny star at each of them, pinning them to a wall. He stepped forward, sizing up which of the three was ripe for questioning. Fear was a powerful motivator.

"Why don't you tell me what's going on here?" Uriel suggested, directing his question to the man he'd met outside. "You seem to be in charge."

"Nothing," the man answered, turning his face to the side.

Uriel pressed down on where the star-shaped blade pierced his skin. "Shall we try that again? What was that ad about?"

A high-pitched whistle passed by his ear. Uriel spun around, but saw no one. He turned back to find all three of his captives dead. A dart was implanted in each of their foreheads – tipped with poison, no doubt. There wasn't time to investigate. A loud bang was reason enough to hit the road. Fire was already out of control by the time he reached the upper level. He raced down the aisles, avoiding falling wood, breaking glass, and flames. Without thinking, he tossed his body through the doorway, hoping for the best. Crashes from behind him mixed with sirens in the distance. Sticking around would only serve to bring himself under further scrutiny. He made a dash for his truck, grabbing his hat from the grass where it still lay, and almost bumping into a couple walking down the sidewalk.

"Sorry," he muttered, keeping his head down. He glanced back over his shoulder. They weren't paying attention to the fire.

The couple paused, swaying slightly as they prepared to cross the street. Their chests heaved up and down in unison, matching their other mechanical movements. Uriel inhaled deeply, filtering out the scent of the fire. It was faint, but there nonetheless: demons. Their movements, however, made no sense. Following, they came to a full stop in front of a music shop two blocks down. Uriel's mind raced. He hadn't seen where the woman he met earlier had gone, but he was willing to bet it was into the Velvet Violin.

Chapter Thirteen

The door was already off its hinges by the time Uriel reached it, lights flickering eerily on the opposite side of the threshold. Fingers slid over course threads, ready to grab his trusty lasso, if the need arose. There was little doubt it would. The gargling noises only demons made drew him in further, sidestepping a knocked over display. A breeze from the door caught strewn papers, lifting them up and distributing them throughout the store. Their edges rustled, imitating the sound of flapping wings. A single hand batted them away.

Hissing from behind joined grumbles ahead. There were more than two demons on the premises. He was surrounded. His rope shifted in circles in one hand, ready for action. The slightest movement would draw his ire.

A shadow. Musical notes. The flying music sheets. The putrid scent of death. Uriel learned how to deal without one of his sense, but not all of them preoccupied at once. He shifted his weight toward a flash of darkness, weapon twirling. A second movement and he let it fly; managing to noisily rope in a cymbal.

"I always wanted to play the drums," Uriel snickered. "For some reason, I always ended up with the triangle." The lasso took flight again, this time hooking a guitar. A single tug brought it down from where it hung on the wall.

"What's going on?" Bekka cried, racing from the backroom. She flicked the lights on. "You." Her mouth dropped. "You're the thief in the area. I'm calling the cops."

Uriel glanced behind him. There was no one there. "You're talking to me?!" he exclaimed. "I was trying to stop the ones who broke in here. I'm the good guy."

"Save it for the judge," Bekka snarled, phone in hand.

Two black eyes appeared from their hiding spot. Before Uriel could move, it was too late. "Look out!" he yelled.

"For what?" Bekka spun around, her hand reaching for a dart lodged in her neck. Eyes rolling backward, her knees buckled, sending her falling to the ground.

The demon howled the victory cries of an entire pack of wolves, freezing a few steps away from the woman's lifeless body.

Uriel glared directly into dead eyes. The rope was already twirling once again. This time, all his senses were focused. This time he wasn't about to miss. The rope took flight, slicing through any papers it touched and easily finding its target. A single pull tightened the hold. It was an easy decision. A demon wasn't about to wag its tongue for a horseman. A second tug sliced the creature in half. The rope fell to the ground. While he enjoyed the playtime, there were more urgent matters to deal with. He was already injured, as was the woman. They both needed to heal. There was only one way that was going to happen. Gun in hand; he fired off shots at the others. They each fell as silent as the night outside. Even the breeze ceased, the papers falling down into piles on the floor, sensing the battle was over and preserving their energy for the war yet to come.

Uriel knelt by the woman. She was alive, but there was no way to know what substance had been on the dart. Whatever was going on was not only bigger than he anticipated; it also revolved around her. If answers were to be had, she needed to live. He scooped her up over his shoulder.

Michael said it was urgent he return. Of course, Uriel knew all too well that meant alone. He chuckled, knowing his brother wasn't going to take kindly to an outsider coming for a visit.

Chapter Fourteen

Bekka's vision blurred, refusing to focus. She moaned, reaching for her head – hoping someone wrote down the licence plate of the truck that hit her. Memories returned in no particular order. The shop being robbed. The dizzy nausea. The room spinning. The cowboy. She rubbed her eyes, hoping to clear away some of the confusion. Her chest heaved up and down, heart racing, at the lack of familiarity around her.

Bekka wanted a strange fantasy adventure, but the past twenty-four hours had been a bit much: strange handsome men, a robbery, a cowboy, and waking up in an old-fashioned castle of some sort. At least that's what the bedroom she was in reminded her of. Her hands smoothed over the velvet surface of the bedspread, before turning their attention to the silk pillow covers. This was her first time in a four-poster bed. It was everything she imagined and more. She flopped back, her eyes drinking in the rest of the sights. Rich, dark hardwood furniture was arranged to make a hearth the focal point of the room. A fire danced wildly in a performance made for one. The crackles of wood beneath smouldering heat provided the only music needed.

Bekka sighed. This was perfect. It was everything she wanted and more. Visions of the elegant gentleman from her shop made the scene complete. Except, he hadn't been there when she was attacked. The only person she saw was the cowboy. A cold sweat formed on her brow. She had been abducted. The door cracked open.

"Hi," Uriel said, wandering in with a cold compress. "I didn't think you'd be up for a while. That stuff knocked you out cold."

"You!" Bekka cried, jumping to her feet. She stammered forward, one hand poised to strike.

A smile crossed Uriel's lips, one hand rubbing his jaw. "Nice shot," he cackled. "Although, it's a strange way to say thank you. If you've got that out of your system, perhaps we can try to figure out who attacked you. Let's go."

"Where are we going?" Bekka complained.

Uriel glanced back at the woman. "To meet my family. You might want to be a bit nicer to them. They don't put up with being slapped around like I do."

"I'm not going anywhere with you until you explain what's going on!" Bekka shrieked.

"See," Uriel began, "that's counterproductive. I'm trying to take you to another room where we can figure out what's going on, and you want to stay here until you have the answers." He shrugged his shoulders. "Stay for all I care. I, myself, need to see if anyone else can help fill in any of the missing details."

Bekka watched him stroll out the door, leaving it open. She peeked around the corner, eyeing the direction he took. This was her chance to either escape or follow. One foot came down hard on the floor, her head shaking. Curiosity was pure evil, but she had to know where the cowboy went and what was going on. She traced his steps, taking in the ageless beauty of the art lining the walls along the way. The path ended at a set of wooden double doors. She breathed in deeply, pulling them open. Her jaw dropped at the stunning library set out before her.

Chapter Fifteen

Uriel mimicked his brother, slouching back in a chair, feet on the table. "Gabby," he said, acknowledging his sister. "How are things?"

Michael's feet banged on the floor. He stood, slamming his chair against the side of the table. "Things," he said, "would be a lot better if you listened to me once in a while."

"What are your feathers all ruffled over?" Uriel questioned. "If it's about the girl, I need to ask her a few questions. A demon knocked her out with some drug. I couldn't take the chance that it might have been poison."

"It's not about the girl," Michael blurted out. "Or rather it's all about the girl."

Uriel chuckled. "Which one is it? It can't be both about her and not about her. Are you feeling okay? Maybe the pressure has been getting to you."

"Enough," Gabby yelled, slamming her hands down on the table. Books bounced up, falling back in place. "Now you've made me lose my spot."

"Um," Bekka said. "Who are you people, and what do you want with me?"

Gabby's scowl turned to a sweet smile. "Hi," she answered. "I'm Gabby, Uriel's sister. I know this must feel like an odd way to meet."

Bekka's lips opened and closed, pursing together. "Who is Uriel?"

Uriel raised his hand. "That would be me."

Michael glanced between them. "You two aren't on a first-name basis yet?" He chuckled under his breath.

"Why would we be?" Bekka asked. "We only spoke once before he decided to rob my store."

Uriel's feet came down hard from their table perch. "I wasn't robbing you. I was trying to stop intruders." He threw his hands up in the air. "This is what I get for being a nice guy."

"A nice guy," Bekka barked. "Try overbearing and egotistical."

"We talking about Michael again?" Ryder joked, strolling in, with Tara right behind. "I can vouch for personality."

"Very funny," Michael scoffed. "You better watch out, Uri, this guy might take your comedian jobs right out from under your feet."

"Who in the heavens are these two?" Uriel questioned. "Are we running a bed and breakfast around here?"

"We were getting to that," Gabrielle replied. "If everyone could please take a seat, I'll go over the details. It's quite the story. I think you two will find it most interesting."

"In the meantime," Michael said. "I'll need some identification." He held out his hand.

Bekka laughed. "Talk to your Neanderthal brother. I wasn't given an opportunity to grab a purse. It's back at my store, or what's left of it, that is." Daggers darted from her eyes in Uriel's direction.

"We'll have to take you at your word," Gabrielle suggested. "What's your name?"

"Bekka."

Ryder crossed his arms over his chest. "This is the best part." He pressed his lips firmly together forming a goofy smile.

"As I was saying, I am Gabrielle. These are two of my brothers, Michael and Uriel." She paused. "We have one other brother, Raphael. Is this ringing any bells for you?"

Bekka shook her head, twitching her lips from side to side. "Nope."

"For the gods' sake, stop pussy-footing around," Michael complained. "We're the four horsemen. I'm sure you've heard of them."

"Nope," Bekka replied, shrugging her shoulders.

"Of the Apocalypse," Ryder added.

"Sorry," Bekka said.

"Okay," Gabrielle said. "How about this? We are demigods fighting evil forces in the world. Our job is to keep the gates to hell closed."

"Sounds like a crappy job," Bekka said. "Sorry for your luck. What does this have to do with me?"

"She isn't the brightest, is she?" Michael blurted out. "I'll spell it out for you. You were attacked by demons and Uriel saved you."

"Why would demons want to attack me?" Bekka questioned.

"That is what we are trying to figure out," Tara explained. "I know this must be difficult for you, but I was attacked by demons too, and Michael saved me."

"So what is it these demons are after?" Bekka asked.

"The keys to the gates of hell," Ryder announced. "They want to unleash whatever is behind those doors. Let me tell you, after coming face-to-face with a bunch of those things, I can say for certain, we don't want that to happen."

"I don't have any keys," Bekka huffed.

"That's the thing," Gabrielle said. "The keys are people."

"What?!" Uriel shrieked. "When did you decide this?"

"What do you think we were trying to tell you?" Michael complained. "If you hadn't hung up on me, you might know these little details."

"I'm a key," Tara announced.

"Me too," Ryder said, waving a hand over his head.

"How do we know who is a key?" Uriel questioned. "Demons attack people all the time, and we've never come to this conclusion before."

"I'm sure you've figured this out," Michael said, nudging his brother with an elbow. His eyebrows waggled suggestively.

"No," Uriel said. "I haven't. How do you know these two are keys? Is there a test of some sort?"

"Because they are our mates," Gabrielle announced.

"What?!" Bekka and Uriel shrieked in unison.

Uriel chuckled. "Who exactly is mates with who here?"

Michael and Gabrielle exchanged glances. "Announcing couple number one, you two," Michael said, alternating pointing his finger between his brother and the newly arrived woman.

Uriel laughed. "No," he said. "We aren't involved."

"Yet," Ryder said, nodding.

"Ever," Bekka announced.

"You can't deny the attraction, though," Tara suggested. "Right?"

"You are way off base," Uriel argued.

"We can prove it," Gabrielle announced. "If Bekka is meant to be your mate, she will be able to use the front door."

Uriel shrugged his shoulders. "Give it a whirl," he said.

"Do you mind?" Gabrielle asked.

"If I do this, can I leave?" Bekka questioned. "I have plans tonight."

"Fine," Gabby answered, motioning for the woman to take the lead. The two headed to the entrance. "Go ahead and open it."

Bekka placed one hand on the handle and pulled. "Is it locked?" she questioned. "Is this some sort of a sick game?"

"No," Gabby replied. "I was so sure." One hand covered her mouth. "It doesn't make any sense. Why would the demons attack you if you weren't one of the keys?" She wandered back to the library.

"I did what you asked," Bekka complained. "You said I could go."

"Told you," Uriel said, eyeing his sister's expression. "Why do I have a feeling there is more to this story than I am being told?"

"It fit the pattern," Gabrielle mumbled.

"What pattern?" Uriel asked, frustration showing signs in his strained voice.

"He only goes after the keys," Gabrielle continued, ignoring her brother.

"Who?" Uriel asked.

"Dante," Michael replied, knowing their sister was lost in thought. "He's the one behind the sudden uprising."

"Dante?!" Uriel said, making a face to match his confusion. "Didn't he die way back? Are you trying to tell me we are fighting a ghost?"

"No," Michael replied. "He's very much alive and playing for the other team now. We haven't figured out what game it is, though. He seems to be dangerous then lenient. One thing we do know is, he wants the gates to hell opened."

"Who's Dante?" Bekka questioned.

Ryder pointed to the picture on display. "That guy. He's a real piece of work... a charmer through and through."

Bekka gazed at the image. The corner of her lips edged upward a smidge. "He's a good-looking man."

"Have you seen him before?" Michael asked.

"No," Bekka lied. "I need to get back to my world. My store was left is a mess and without a front door. Now that I'm not some weird living key, I may not matter to you, but I still have a life to live."

"You may not be out of danger," Michael suggested. "Demons don't pick random targets. They wanted something."

"I'll take my chances," Bekka snapped. "Take me back."

Uriel nodded. "I'll stick around town for a bit to make sure things smooth over. That's the best we can offer you. If you can think of anything that they might have wanted."

"An artifact?" Gabby blurted out.

Uriel shifted his weight, inching forward. "Come to think of it, there was mention of an artifact in the advertisement." He turned his attention to Bekka. "You wouldn't own anything unusual, would you?"

"It would be old," Gabby added. "Possibly handed down through generations in your family. It could have something to do with art or music."

Bekka pursed her lips together, shaking her head. "No, nothing like that," she lied. "All I have is my shop. Sorry I can't help."

"That's okay," Gabby said, offering a meek grin. "We'll figure it out. Are you sure you want to go back so soon?"

"I have bills," Bekka said. "I am hoping that the store wasn't too badly damaged. I might lose everything."

"I'll help you clean it up," Uriel offered. "Let's go." He turned to his siblings. "I'll be back in a few days. Let me know if you figure anything out."

"Keep your phone on," Michael called after them. "We can't talk to you if you shut it off."

Chapter Sixteen

Uriel shoved his hands in his pockets, hanging back a dozen paces. Even that was too close. She was a real piece of work and he had no interest in applying for the job. The more she opened her mouth; the more he cringed, slouching his shoulders and pretending they weren't together – not that she noticed. Her *it's all about me* attitude was wearing thin on his nerves.

"It's fixed!" Bekka exclaimed at the first sight of her shop. She bolted for the door; not worrying that danger might have been lurking nearby.

Uriel rubbed the back of his neck. His long legs meant there was no need to break into a jog to catch up. He simply picked up the pace to a brisk walk. At first sight, the exterior of the music store looked exactly as it had before the demon intrusion. Upon closer inspection, however, many of the parts had been completely replaced.

"Do you know who would have done this?" Uriel questioned, side-eyeing the woman beside him. "It could be a trap."

Bekka's nose curled upward. "Why would someone go through the trouble of fixing it to set a trap? Wouldn't it be easier to leave it and wait inside? They had to know I was coming back. Or perhaps you all are of the opinion smashing things is the best way to handle your differences."

Uriel pushed her to one side. "A broken door in daylight would draw attention," he explained. "This way, no one would be the wiser as to what happened last night. We are of the opinion the less the general public knows about us, the better. That goes for both sides."

"Or it could simply be someone being nice," Bekka snorted. "I do have a few friends who think highly of me, you know." She pulled out a key and held it in front of his face. "I'm going to unlock it now."

Uriel stepped by her the moment the door opened, leaving Bekka to disable the alarm and flick on the lights. He stood in the centre of the room, hands planted firmly on his hips. Fingers tapped on his sides, only an inch away from his lasso. It wasn't needed, though. There was no sign of intruders, or the scuffle from the previous evening.

"Where'd the bodies go?" Uriel questioned. "And the papers?"

Bekka shrugged her shoulders, her eyes locked on the box containing her dress for that evening's gala. "No clue," she answered. "But, as you can see, there is no one here and nothing for me to be afraid of. I appreciate the escort. You can go now." Her hand swayed through the air, shooing him away.

"I don't think you are safe..."

"I said you can go!" Bekka's voice rose. "I have plans and I won't have you ruining them. You've done your good deed for the day, and hopefully made your demon quota last night... or whatever you call it."

"Ma'am," Uriel said, tipping his hat, "I'd like to say it's been a pleasure, but I'd be lying." He shook his head, taking one last glance around the room. Not a smidge of damage was to be seen. The displays were back together and restocked. There also wasn't a drop of blood on the floor. To accomplish that in such a short period of time would have taken a major clean-up crew. It also wasn't something demons could manage on their own. With the destruction of the local chapter, it was unlikely local followers were involved. Whoever fixed the store was an outsider.

*****

Bekka watched Uriel leave, before bolting to the backroom. One foot tapped on the secret compartment, before she bent over to open it. Her heart raced. The violin had been an important part of the history of her family, but she had never realized exactly how valuable it was. One hand covered her chest at the sight of the case and book, untouched. She let out the air she had been holding in one big huff.

A chuckle escaped her partly open lips. Lying before her was the best thing to ever happen to her. It was a bargaining chip – all she needed to figure out was how to use it to her advantage. Her fingers flipped through the pages of the book, ending on the explanation for her lineage. For years she'd been nothing but a decoy; her parents switching her at birth with another baby. She'd never understood why, until that moment. Demons! They were protecting Veronica from them all this time. She shook her head. Her own life meant so little to so many, but that was about to change. They'd tasked her with protecting the sacred artifact without knowledge. She was in control of what happened to it now. The trapdoor slammed shut, the book remaining in her hands.

There was no doubt in her mind, the man from the conservatory and this Dante were one and the same. Uriel might have flexed his muscle, but Dante had shown he had so much more to offer, and it was true power. He had money, clout, and the right connections. Before the night was out, she planned to take some of it for herself.

Chapter Seventeen

Bekka glanced at her own reflection in the window, swaying and swooshing her dress from side to side. She'd managed to fit in a trip to the salon for a proper up-do and manicure. All she lacked was her date. She glanced at her watch, biting on her bottom lip. Excitement was hard to contain. She'd stepped outside and locked to door precisely on time. It was her date who was fashionably late. Her arms crossed over her chest, one foot tapping.

"Where are you?" she grumbled.

As if on cue, a black limousine pulled up. The driver dashed around the hood, opening the door. He motioned with one hand for her to enter the back.

"Good evening," Dante said, peeking out the open door. "Please join me." He lifted a glass of champagne. "It's a wonderful year and I do hate to drink alone."

A smile crept over Bekka's lips as she accepted his offer. The door shut before she was fully seated. "Thank you," she said, grasping the flute being offered. "This is a beautiful car."

Dante chuckled. "I'm glad you like it."

"Don't you?" Bekka asked; her eyes filled with the wonder of a child on Christmas morning.

"It serves its purposes," Dante replied, allowing champagne to tickle his lips after the last word. "How are you, my dear?"

"Fine," Bekka answered. "I expect that I owe you a debt of gratitude for fixing my shop after I was attacked last night."

"No need," Dante chuckled, holding up one hand.

"No, really," Bekka insisted. "Thank you, Dante. It is Dante, isn't it?" Her lips curled into a sly grin. "I saw a picture of you from long ago."

"I see," Dante replied, placing his glass in a holder. "So you think you know who I am." His lips pursed together. "I suppose you met my four friends as well?"

"I met three," Bekka admitted, "Although, I would use the term friend loosely. It seems you are on opposite sides of the pond, at the moment."

Dante laughed. "Right you are," he said. "I have to wonder why you are here if they told you everything."

"There are two sides to every story," Bekka answered. "I prefer your approach to things, except for the muscle exercised last night, of course."

"I assure you, that wasn't my doing," Dante commented. "The parties involved have all been dealt with. I promise you it won't happen again."

"I suppose you would like to get down to business," Bekka suggested.

The limousine came to a halt, the driver opening the back door. "Ah!" Dante exclaimed. "We are here. Why don't we leave business until after the gala? I have been looking forward to a night out dancing. It wouldn't be fair to deprive the other guests of your beauty. Did I mention how stunning you look this evening?"

"No, you didn't," Bekka replied, accepting his hand to help her from the back seat. She latched on to the crook of his elbow, taking in the magnificence of her surroundings. There hadn't been any galas or balls in her life before. In fact, the last time she'd danced with anyone had been in her junior year of high school. She shivered at the thought.

"Don't worry, my dear," Dante whispered. "Follow my steps. I won't lead you astray. Dancing may take two people, but only one needs to know how."

The tone of his voice soothed her nerves. She nodded her understanding, unable to form words. The sheer magnitude of the party before her was more frightening than any concert recital.

"Keep breathing," Dante instructed, his smile never faltering. A twinkle in his eye greeted each and every person they passed with the same warmth she experienced by his side. He presented an invitation to security at a set of double doors, leading into a grand ballroom. "Thank you. Shall we, my dear? The band has already warmed up."

Inside the room was a complete sensory overload. An orchestra played in the background, with groups talking over top of the music. Couples swung around in circles on the dance floor, while the scent of a buffet stocked full of finger foods beckoned her to try each and every one. They would have to wait, though. Her mind was fixed on fashion. Each woman wore a beautiful gown worthy of a red carpet, her own rivalling the finest of them. A slew of colours whizzed by her eyes, forming a distorted rainbow on the dance floor. Through it all she hadn't heard a word that had been said directly beside her.

Dante's arm encircled her back, spinning her without warning. "Very good," he said, pulling her close. "That was your first dance lesson. Count this a part two." A mischievous grin spanned his face as he led her around the room.

"Sorry," Bekka muttered, glancing down at their feet.

"Sh," Dante hushed in her ear. "The only one who knows you stepped on my toes is me. No one is watching our feet. I'm not complaining, but if you do, it will draw attention to our errors. Dancing is a type of illusion. Few are truly masters of it. Eyes on me."

Bekka smiled. He wasn't wrong. All the time she had spent admiring the couples moving in perfect time with the rhythm of the music, not once did she look at their feet. It was all about their posture and faces. The happier the couple appeared, the better they seemed to be at dancing. That connection was what took two people years to master. It was all about trusting each other not to point out the other's flaws, rather than a need to learn the steps perfectly.

The orchestra took a break after a few more songs and not a moment too soon. Bekka could feel the beginnings of a light perspiration forming on the back of her neck and face. Some might have called it a healthy shine or a womanly glow. She wasn't one of them. To her it was a warning: stop now or sweat comes next.

Dante again appeared to read her mind. "Would you like a drink?" he asked.

"Please," she answered, following him to the bar. "Is it that obvious?"

"It's nothing more than a healthy flush," Dante snickered. "You'll find it is quite common when attending these events. The rooms tend to have few windows and it can quickly become quite hot from all the bodies. That's why it's a cash bar." He pulled out a wad of bills held together by a silver clip, tossing a couple at a bartender. He raised two fingers. A good tip was the only way to get service at the overcrowded station. Given the level of noise buzzing about, there also wasn't much choice on the menu. They would have to make due with whatever they were given. Dante handed Bekka the first cup, before taking a sip of the second.

His face turned sour. "Good gods!" he exclaimed. "That's terrible." He removed the glass from her grip before even a taste could be had. "Trust me, I am doing you a favour. I think we should head back to the car for a proper beverage." He pulled her hand to his arm, patting it once in place.

"Leaving so soon?" a man questioned.

"I'm afraid so," Dante replied. "It's been a wonderful evening. I hope to see you next month at the art gallery."

"Indeed." The man bowed, stepping aside.

"You've been seen, now," Dante said. "There will be any number of men looking to escort you to such parties and quite a few invitations to concerts. Make the most of them."

"You act as if we are saying goodbye," Bekka pouted.

"Not at all," Dante replied. "We are only beginning to understand each other. Ah, good! I see the car is waiting." He motioned for her to enter first.

"Are we at the business part of the evening?" Bekka questioned, watching her date add ice and water to two glasses. He handed her one. "Thank you."

Dante nodded. "You are relentless," he said. "Tell me what is this business you so desperately want to discuss?"

"Let's not beat around the bush," Bekka suggested. "I know I have something you want."

"Really?" Dante replied, pursing his lips together. "And what, exactly, would that be?"

"I told you I didn't want to play games," Bekka complained. She opened the snap on her hand purse, tossing a notebook on his lap. "I didn't understand it all until I met Uriel and his brood. They pretty much filled in the blanks I'd lived my entire life with. I am not the key."

"You seem pretty sure of that," Dante said, glancing through the handwritten journal. "This is recorded by your family?"

"It was recorded by who I thought was my family," Bekka replied. "There is a section that speaks of the switching of two babies at birth."

Dante gaze darted to meet hers. "You're a decoy?" he questioned. "I have to admit that is a brilliant plan. I never would have known if you hadn't told me. So what is it exactly that you have? If you are not the key, why do I need you?"

"You mean other than to track down the real key?" Bekka asked, chuckling.

"Yes," Dante replied, taking a swig of his water. He refilled the glass. "Other than that."

"Because I have the violin that goes with that journal," she announced. "I have the artifact you want so badly."

"And you are willing to trade it for what?" Dante questioned.

"All my life I've played second fiddle," Bekka commented. "I want to be the star. I want to be the centre of attention."

"And so you shall," Dante agreed. "We have a deal. Now, where can we find that violin?"

"It's back at the shop," Bekka admitted.

Dante rapped on the partition, it opened slightly. "Take us back to the music store please," he ordered. "We are in a hurry." The glass closed again. Dante turned to his date. "Where can I find the real key?"

"I think I have a way to deliver you both at the same time," Bekka replied.

Chapter Eighteen

Uriel sat on a perch hidden from view. He'd wandered around trying to figure out a plan, but in every scenario he ended back up at the music store. It was his one clue in whatever sinister plan was being hatched.

Dante. Uriel's mind wandered back to all the battles they fought side by side. He wasn't as close to the man as his siblings had been, but he had called him a friend nonetheless. The day Dante fell was etched into each of their psyches – a dark blemish that could never be erased. He carried his own scars for many years, dealing with them in his own way. If what his brother and sister said was true, the crude homemade stitches were about to be torn apart. Dante becoming a traitor was salt poured in the wound.

A breeze carried a subtle message. Uriel's nostrils widened, awaiting news of malice and deceit, but something else was hidden within the air. A sweet scent he'd come across a few times – honeysuckle. Closing his eyes, he could have basked in the warmth of the honey and citrus notes for eternity. With them open, however, a woman ruined the picture. Bekka's personality simply didn't match the fragrance.

Days had gone by since the music store had last opened. The first sight of auburn hair blowing in the wind had Uriel on his feet, ready to pounce. Her disappearance had something to do with whatever plan had been set into motion in the city. His arm reached out tapping her shoulder.

"Who are you?" she cried, turning around and inching back a few steps. "What do you want?"

"Sorry," Uriel answered, holding his hands palms first in front of him. "I thought you were the owner of the music store. You have the same colour hair."

"What do you want her for?" the woman asked.

"I just wanted to talk," Uriel replied.

"You're the cowboy she met the other day," the woman blurted out. "You have something to do with Bekka's disappearance, don't you?"

Uriel eyed the woman up and down. "You are the woman in the demon worshippers' yard. The one who was being attacked. Who are you?"

"I could ask you the same thing," she barked. "Things got strange from the moment you showed up."

"I'm Uriel," he said. "I am trying to find Bekka. I think she may be in trouble. The man you were with the other evening, did you know him well?"

"No," the woman answered. "I met him on an online dating app. It was our first," she rolled her eyes, "and last date."

"It would be easier if I knew your name," Uriel suggested.

"Veronica," she replied. "Bekka is more than my best friend. She's like a sister to me. We grew up together. We were even born in the same hospital on the same day. Our parents were good friends, too."

"When was the last time you heard from her?" Uriel asked.

"Days ago," Veronica admitted, sniffling. "We had a fight. We never fight." Tears fell freely down her face, pooling in the dimple on her chin before dripping off one at a time. "This is the longest we have gone without talking. I'm worried something has happened to her."

Uriel fought the urge to wipe the tears from her face, but when she broke into a full sob, it was game over. He pulled her into an embrace, offering his shoulder as a towel for her sadness. "It's okay," he whispered. "We'll find her."

"How?" Veronica questioned, her breathing erratic from weeping.

"Does she have any family?" Uriel asked.

Veronica shook her head, rubbing makeup off on his shirt. "No." The word came with a new round of wailing. "Our parents all passed away."

"What about friends?" Uriel questioned.

Veronica pulled away. "All we have is each other. That's all we have ever had. I don't know what I'd do if something happened to her."

"Sh," Uriel hushed her. "Nothing bad is going to happen." He took in a deep breath, wondering why he was lying to a woman he had just met. He had no reason to feel an attachment to her, but still he couldn't bring himself to tell her what his heart already knew – something bad had already happened.

"How do you know?" Veronica questioned. "I watch television. I know after forty-eight hours the trail goes cold."

"I want you to think of places she liked visiting," Uriel instructed. "Can you do that? If you have something to write them down on even better."

Veronica searched her purse, finding a pack of tissues first. After blowing her nose louder than a trumpet a few times, she returned to the original hunt. It wasn't ideal, but she came up with an envelope from a bill and an eyeliner. She sat down on a concrete step. The end of the pencil tapped on her forehead, teeth biting her bottom lip. As many times as she pressed the tip to the paper, she removed it again as well. Not a single word was written. Her brows furrowed, a scowl forming on her face.

"This is the only place she went," Veronica finally admitted. "She isn't very good with people."

"You don't say," Uriel answered, biting his tongue as to his own dislike of the woman. "Still, she runs a shop."

"She loves music," Veronica said. "It was her life. She could have given up everything else, as long as she could play the violin."

"The violin," Uriel repeated. "Why own a music store? Why not play in an orchestra or a band even?"

"Because it meant playing for people," Veronica replied. "Everything is fine until you throw in socializing. If she went anywhere, she needed someone to go along and handle the talking for her. You saw first-hand how she was when you spoke to her."

"I'm not sure that was simply being socially awkward," Uriel suggested. "When we first spoke it was amusing, but the next time she was down right spiteful."

"She is just misunderstood," Veronica cried. "I know her. Deep down she is a sweet person. Everyone has one mental issue or another these days. It takes time to understand them and look past them."

"Although, that's excellent advice," Uriel said, rubbing his chin. He hadn't had time for a shave at the house. A beard in any form was a bad look for him, unless he planned on dressing up like a leprechaun at Halloween. "I'm not sure it helps us at the moment." A ringing sound interrupted his words.

Veronica held up one finger, gazing at her cell phone. "It's Bekka's number," she whispered. Her finger swiped the screen, putting it on speaker. "Hello."

"Veronica, it's me," Bekka said.

"Bekka!" Veronica exclaimed. "Where are you? I've been worried sick. You haven't opened the music store in days and no one has been at your place." Her words quickened as she spoke.

"I need your help," Bekka cried. "You have to do exactly what I say. I need you to use the spare key and go into the shop. The code for the alarm is our birthday. Enter it then head to the backroom. Beneath the mat there is a trapdoor."

"What is this all about?" Veronica questioned. "Where are you?"

"Listen to me," Bekka demanded. "Inside the locket my mom and dad gave you is a key. Use it to open the lock."

"What's inside, Bekka?" Veronica asked.

"A violin," Bekka replied. "It's very old."

"What am I going to do with it?" Veronica asked, her voice shaking.

"You are going to trade it for my life," Bekka said. "Get it now, then head east out of the city. Wait for another call with further details on where to go. If anything goes wrong, they'll kill me. Please, Veronica. You are the only one I can trust."

The phone went dead. "Bekka! Bekka!" Veronica screeched.

Uriel took the phone from her hand. "Let's get this violin," he suggested. "I'll drive you. Wherever she is, we'll find her."

"If something goes wrong," her voice trembled. "I should go alone."

"Even if you could manage to drive in your condition, I wouldn't let you by yourself," Uriel said. "This is too dangerous. Besides, she never said you had to come alone." He winked, adding a reassuring smile.

Chapter Nineteen

Uriel quickly cleaned up the papers and tabloids from the front of his truck. He wasn't used to having a passenger and it showed. He brushed off the seat, before offering Veronica a hand up. After she was safely belted in, he passed her the violin. He had taken a brief look at it, basically only long enough to verify its age. Music wasn't his specialty. He enjoyed listening to it, but technicalities were beyond his knowledge. Gabrielle would have been able to pinpoint the exact season, year, and place the instrument was made. He nailed it down to before such instruments became mainstream.

Veronica opened the case and stared at the instrument, her fingers tracing over the wood. "It's beautiful," she mumbled.

"Bekka never told you about it before?" Uriel questioned.

"No," Veronica said, side-eyeing her driver. Her eyes lingered a smidge too long in some places, bringing a smile to his face. She glanced away, hiding an obvious blush. "We never had any secrets. I don't understand any of this."

"Ma'am," Uriel started.

"Call me Veronica, please."

"Okay, Veronica," Uriel continued, "you may have to accept that you don't know everything about Bekka. I have a gut feeling things aren't as they seem. I'm going to need you to listen to me if we encounter any trouble. I don't want you to get hurt." He winced at the words. He'd gone from a joke-toting cowboy to a tongue-tied fool in a matter of minutes. There must have been something in that perfume.

"I can't," Veronica replied, eyes tearing up in preparation for blubbering number two of the day. "I refuse to believe that she was hiding anything from me on purpose. We don't have secrets."

"Except the violin and you, yourself, said she was acting strange as of late," Uriel reminded. "What sort of things has she been doing differently?"

"You think it could be body snatchers?!" Veronica exclaimed. "She was always reading those tabloids. The same ones you had here in the truck. Are you an alien hunter?"

"Not exactly," Uriel replied, arching one brow. "Were the tabloids new for Bekka, or did she always read them?"

"Not as new as other things," Veronica admitted. "She started copying me. That was a bit eerie."

"Copying in what way?" Uriel asked.

"Buying similar clothes," Veronica replied. "We stopped with the matching hairstyles in grade school, then suddenly one day, hers was the same as mine again. She even started wearing the same perfume as me."

That explained the fragrances. "It suits you more," Uriel commented. "It also sounds as if she was a bit jealous of you."

"No!" Veronica exclaimed, waving one hand through the air. "Why would she be jealous of me? It's not as if I have my life together. If anything, Bekka is more stable than I am. I always have my head in the air looking for something magical to happen... love at first sight and all that." A nervous chuckle followed her words.

"There is nothing wrong with that," Uriel said, not knowing if he was reassuring her or himself. A quick glance in her direction made him a true believer.

The phone rang. Veronica swiped the screen, sending the caller directly to speaker. "Hello," she answered.

"You should be approaching a side road. Turn left. Follow it until you come to a dirt road on the right. Continue for twenty minutes to a deserted farmhouse. Pull around back to the barns." The man hung up before another word could be spoken.

"Looks like we have a destination," Uriel said, arching his eyebrows. "It's well off the beaten path, too."

"What does that mean?" Veronica asked.

"There won't be any witnesses," Uriel replied. He held his gaze on the road; worried he wouldn't be able to handle the sight of fear in Veronica's eyes.

Chapter Twenty

For most of the trip, the outside world was not only flat, but also golden as far as the eye could see. Even if there were land rolls, they were hidden by crops – a grain of some sort, perhaps wheat. Somewhere along the way, well-kept fields turned wild. Yellow mixed with green, weeds spouting like a disease, strangling out that which was intended to grow.

Dust, partially hid Veronica's view, spinning up from beneath the tires. Every bump was an additional reminder of what they had left behind: civilization and pavement. Her car never would have made it, most likely bottoming out a few miles back.

Pressure built in her nose. Sneezes always came at the most inopportune times. She sniffed back, trying to take control, but only managing to intensify the need. Her hand raced forward, covering her mouth just in time. "Ah-choo." Red raced to her cheeks. It wasn't proper to use a hand anymore. She should have remembered to use the crease of her elbow. It was too late now, though. He'd already seen her faux pas.

"There's tissues in the glove compartment," Uriel said, side-eyeing her.

Veronica felt his gaze. It was warmer than a tanning bed on full blast and had the same effect. Her skin was red all over. "Excuse me," she mumbled. "I'm a city girl born and raised. I'm not used to this much fresh air."

Uriel let out a hearty chuckle. "I don't think you are allergic to fresh air. It's most likely the pollen. The less you are exposed to certain allergens at a young age, the more likely you are to develop an allergy when you first encounter them."

"Great," Veronica sighed. "I guess we won't be sneaking up on anyone." She paused taking in a few breaths leading to a second, louder sneeze.

"Probably not," Uriel snorted. "But they knew we were coming anyway. I didn't think we were going to do too much sneaking."

"Ah-choo," Veronica sneezed. "This is worse than a cold. Please tell me it won't last as long as one."

"No," Uriel replied. "It should clear up when you are away from the fresh air." He rolled his eyes. "Once you're back in the smog of the city, you'll feel much better."

"Very funny," Veronica huffed, her eyes watering and nose turning red. "I guess I need to live in the city, though. I couldn't function like this."

"Not necessarily," Uriel replied. "It depends on what is causing you to sneeze. First you have to pinpoint it and then figure out if you can build a tolerance to it on your own. There are shots now for those who can't, too."

"I don't sneeze around flowers," Veronica admitted. She glanced out the window at purple blooms all but hidden behind the cloud of dust being kicked up by spinning tires. "Dust."

"Could be." Uriel turned the fan to air conditioning. "Whatever it is, this should help."

A blast of cool air hit her face. She breathed in deeply, sniffling. "I feel defective," Veronica admitted.

"Don't," Uriel said. "We all have one thing or another that's weird about us."

"Oh yeah," Veronica snorted. "What's yours?"

"For starters, I can't wear a watch," Uriel replied. "They either break or go haywire. I end up with a scaly spot on my wrist. It's horrid."

"I don't like watches either," Veronica admitted. "Actually, I prefer not to wear most jewellery. I think it reacts with my skin in some strange chemical way. I end up with a greenish tinge where any metal touches me for extended periods of time. Does that sound horrid?"

"Not at all," Uriel replied, smiling. "I know exactly what you mean." He nodded at a building they were approaching.

"Is that it?" Veronica asked, her nose crinkling up. "It looks like it's seen a few better days. I wouldn't count on it being safe."

"That's the way they want it to look," Uriel replied. "That way no one comes snooping." He pulled in the long winding driveway and coasted to the back lot. A series of barns sat a few hundred feet away. "Guess that's where we are heading. Bring the violin. I'd like to get the exchange over with and you two girls out of here quickly. I'm leaving my keys in the truck. When you have Bekka, head back here and go. Don't look back."

"What about you?!" Veronica exclaimed, her voice cracking.

"Don't worry about me, ma'am," Uriel replied, winking. "This is what I live for. It's time for me to earn my pay."

Veronica stared at him for a moment. "What in the world is that supposed to mean? I know you were trying to be all serious, but you need to work on your macho routine a little. Are you even a real cowboy?"

"No, ma'am, I'm not," Uriel admitted, tipping his hat. "If I make it out of this, maybe I'll explain everything."

"Great," Veronica huffed, jumping out of the truck. "Excuse me if I don't hold my breath for that explanation."

"Just run for it if you get the chance, okay?" Uriel suggested.

"No arguments here." Veronica agreed. "I don't plan to stick around anything that makes me sneeze this much for long. Ah-choo!"

Chapter Twenty-One

The silence was almost perfect. A single cricket ruined it. Once it sang for them, other performers couldn't resist. Soon an army of bugs was trying to outperform each other, in a deafening game of What's That Tune. Uriel dimmed the tune in his mind, allowing his vision to take point. That was his strongest skill, even if it did come with its flaws. The main one was line of sight. If he had an extra set facing behind him, things would have been much easier. His mind wandered to his siblings. Having one of them there to watch his back would have been ideal. He didn't though.

Uriel allowed himself a single glance at Veronica. As much as he was enjoying her company, she didn't belong there. There was a danger lurking on the horizon that he wasn't sure he could protect her from – heck – he wasn't sure he could protect himself. Dante was no ordinary mercenary – the man had skills that rivalled any of the horsemen. There had been a time when he joked about making Dante an official fifth member of the team. Then the accident happened

– a long fall from a cliff during battle. The body was never found.

"What are we doing?" Veronica whispered slowly.

Uriel motioned for her to stay hidden where she was, scrunched down behind a couple of rusty metal barrels. He peeked his head around the tail end of the truck, surveying the area. "Bare bones," he muttered under his breath. That was all that was left – a skeleton of what a farm should be. Remains of buildings showed the signs of years of endurance. Harsh weather had taken its toll on them and no one had bothered with repairs. Instead it had been left to rot. He knelt by a back tire, examining the tracks it left in the dry ground. Other than their own tracks, there was no sign anyone else had come or gone for an extremely long time. That was a bad sign.

Uriel inhaled, deeply, searching for scents to confirm his theory. The absence of animal odours was the only conclusion. He waited for a breeze to make a second attempt. The results were the same. A total lacking, not only of the smells normally associated with an active farm, but in general. His nostrils drew a complete blank. He took another glance at his surroundings. The missing stretch of decay was another red flag.

The meeting was looking more and more like an ambush by the minute. He licked his lips. The abandoned farm wasn't going to have visitors anytime soon. That meant they were alone if something went wrong. Uriel side-eyed his companion again, his intuition insisting he send her packing back to town. The intense determination etched on her face told him she wasn't about to abandon her friend. It was an admirable quality to have – stupid – but admirable.

Uriel sighed. Answers weren't going to pop up and bite him on the nose. He needed to take a closer look at the barns to know what condition they were in. If they were actually in as bad a state as they appeared, no one was going inside. He stepped out from behind the truck, motioning for Veronica to remain where she was.

Uriel only needed to move a few paces closer to know things weren't as they were pretending to be. All it took was a good artist to reconstruct a ghost farm. He tugged on the barn door, opening it enough to squeeze through.

Inside, darkness stole the show. Gaps in the building's frame allowed beams of light through, creating the criss-cross pattern similar to the laser beams a high-security facility might use, albeit he made no attempt to step over or duck under them.

Uriel squatted beside a pile of hay, picking up a handful and letting it fall to the ground again. It wasn't describable as fresh, but it also wasn't old enough to match the appearance of the rest of the farm. He bit his bottom lip. The answer was there somewhere, but it eluded him. He stood, bushing his hands together to remove the remnants of hay and dirt.

A ladder, leading to the loft, caught his attention. He grabbed the handles, shaking them. The wood cracked and creaked, splinters flying from the simple back and forth motion. It wouldn't hold any weight. A shrill scream made him spin around, his heart racing.

Uriel shook his head at Veronica, wincing at a rodent. It scurried away out the open door, more frightened by Veronica than she was of it. "I told you to stay outside," he complained. His hand scratched at his neck. The feeling was one he hadn't felt in decades, but he knew exactly what it meant. He'd been drugged by a prick. A smile crossed his face at his own pun. *Dante!*

The room spun. Uriel locked his gaze on Veronica, trying to ease the dizziness. It was too late, though. Even his lips were too numb to form a sentence. Instead he forced one word from them. "Run!"

Uriel stammered toward Veronica, trying to shoo her out the door. His legs wobbled, knees buckling. Darkness followed.

Chapter Twenty-Two

"Uriel! Uriel!"

That voice – he knew that voice. Uriel begged his eyelids to open. It made no difference, though. His eyes rolled back, looking inside his own mind instead of at who was calling his name. Pain radiated through his temple. The first attempt to reach up failed, only a single finger responding to the command. On the second attempt, he felt resistance.

"What the..."

"You're tied up," a sweet voice sang in his ear. Blurry vision refused to clear. It was a woman sitting beside him, her outline glowing with light.

"You tied me up, angel?" he smirked, chuckling. "That's a bad girl. Why don't you let me loose?" His final words slurred.

"You sound drunker than a college student during frosh week!" Veronica complained. "Snap out of it. We are in trouble!"

"Trouble," Uriel answered, laughing. "What sort of trouble could we be in? I feel fine."

"What did they give you?" Veronica asked. "And why didn't I get any?"

"Because," a man said, entering the room. A buzzer sounded as the door shut behind him. "It would have killed you."

"What?!" Veronica shrieked, glancing between the two men. "Who are you? What do you want with us? Where is Bekka?"

The man held up a hand. "One question at a time, please. It's all I can answer." He pulled a chair across the room, allowing the feet to scratch the floor. Facing the back toward them, he straddled it, sitting. "Allow me to introduce myself..."

"Dante!" Uriel exclaimed. "I thought you were dead! Are you a ghost?"

Dante sighed. "I see it hasn't completely worn off yet," he said, chuckling. "Uriel, you always were the life of the party. Looks like you will be the entertainment one more time."

"I'd shake your hand," Uriel said, head swaying. "But they don't seem to want to move." He motioned for his old friend to move closer with his head. Lowering his voice to a whisper he continued, "She says she tied me up." He howled a laugh.

Dante alternated his glance between them. "She did, did she?"

Veronica sighed. "I wish I could do a face palm right now." Her wrists wriggled under the constriction of her own bonds.

"As I was saying," Dante continued, clearing his throat. "I am Dante." He paused, shrugging his shoulders. The words were less impressive after Uriel had already provided the information.

"Funny," Veronica snapped. "I figured that answer out already. How about you tell me why I'm tied up and what you did to Uriel?"

"Uriel will be fine," Dante blurted out. "It's a special concoction that a scientist made to subdue one of his kind."

"His kind?" Veronica repeated.

"My goodness, I thought you would know at least a little about things. Hasn't he told you who he is?" Dante waggled a finger back and forth. "Tsk-tsk."

"We don't go around telling everyone we meet," Uriel said, a silly grin plastered to his face.

"That's no way to treat your mate, Uriel," Dante complained. "Your hearts might be destined, but you should still treat her with respect."

"Mate?" Uriel questioned, both eyebrows trying to rise at different times. "She's not my mate."

"Really, then tell me who is?" Dante questioned.

"Bekka!" Uriel blurted. "I love Bekka. Is she here? I would really... really... really like to see her." An overworked wink ended his words, one that required mouth movements as well. Drool fell from his lips, landing on his lap. He continued his laughter.

Dante pulled on the whiskers forming on his chin, eyes darting from side-to-side. "Interesting," he mumbled. "This changes things." He stood tossing the chair at the wall. "You two stay cozy. I'll be back."

"Where's Bekka?" Veronica yelled after him. Her whole body tugged against her restraints in vain. "Ah!"

"Save your strength," Uriel muttered.

"Save my strength," Veronica cried. "Save my strength. Easy to say when you are higher than a kite."

Uriel glanced over. "I'm fine," he said. "I was buying a bit of time. I could tell Dante wanted to have some big conversation before making a move. He wants me alert. Nothing will happen until after that.

"Do you have a plan?" Veronica questioned.

"That's why I needed time," Uriel replied. "To come up with one. Can you tell me what happened?"

"Not really," Veronica admitted. "They put a sack over my head. I couldn't see a thing."

"Don't concentrate on what you saw," Uriel said. "Did you hear anything? How many people were holding you? One or one on each arm?"

"One, I think," Veronica answered, her voice shaking. "No there were two... one on each side. And one was in front of them, giving orders."

"Good," Uriel praised. "Did they put us in a vehicle?"

"No," Veronica answered. "No we walked a ways, then there was a noise; metal on metal."

"What happened next?" Uriel pried.

"I don't know," Veronica said. "We walked forward two steps and stood there. I felt a jerk. Then they turned me around to go back the way we came. Next thing I knew, I was in this room. I'm not much help."

"More than you know," Uriel said. "We are under the farm. That helps when we need to find our way back up again."

"Can you break the straps?" Veronica asked.

"I'm trying," Uriel admitted. "It's made of some form of metal I haven't come across before."

"If you can't, we aren't going anywhere."

He could hear every tear trickling down her face. "Don't worry. There is always a Plan B."

"Care to share?" Veronica asked in a shaky voice.

"I will," Uriel replied, "as soon as I think of it."

"That's not very reassuring," Veronica said. "We are going to die here, aren't we? At least tell me why!"

"You wouldn't believe me if I did," Uriel blurted out, his muscles tensed. Clenching his teeth together he pulled up, using every bit of strength he had. The restraints remained in place. There wasn't so much as a wiggle. His head leaned back. It didn't make any sense. He'd never met a metal he couldn't bend before. All his efforts were merely wasted. It was time for Plan B and that required Dante's return.

Chapter Twenty-Three

Little by little, Uriel's senses completely returned to normal. He heard the click of the door locks before it opened. The tugging and wriggling resumed, adding in a few huffs and puffs for show.

"Ah," Dante said. "I see you are much more alert now." A second chair scraped along the floor. "You are wasting your time."

"Forgive me if I don't take your word for it," Uriel snapped.

"By all means," Dante said. "I thought you should know, it's indestructible. You can thank your brother and sister for that. Didn't they mention it?"

"No," Uriel snarled, "they left that part out. I'm sure you will fill me in on the details, though."

"It's a new form of metal," Dante explained, pulling a pack of cigarettes from his jacket pocket. "Do you mind?"

"Yes!" Veronica exclaimed. "I mind very much."

Dante returned the pack from whence it came. "Sorry. Smoking keeps me focused, especially at times like this. What was I saying?" Ah, yes... the metal. Michael broke the prototype quite easily. It was a complete failure. The scientists developing it had to start over. They improved it considerably before my meeting with your sister. Gabrielle is quite frightening, as I'm sure you already know. Where there is a will, there is a way. Her will was unwavering. It took a bit of time, but she broke the second batch. What binds you is the third. We both know you are the weakest link in the group. I am confident you won't be able to break it."

"What is this about, Dante?" Uriel questioned. "There is more to this than revenge. I don't know who you blame for what happened."

Dante howled a laugh, which echoed eerily through the room. "Revenge. An interesting thought. Do you blame yourself for my death?"

"No," Uriel snapped. "Not at all. I was too far away to reach you. What happened was unfortunate, but it was only one person's fault – your own. If anything, I wonder why you tossed years of combat experience aside that day. You knew the danger of fighting too close to a ledge, yet you backed yourself against it."

"Interesting," Dante said. "I always took you as nothing more than comic relief. It seems I may have underestimated you. Not to worry, though. It won't change the outcome of things."

"And what will that be?" Uriel questioned. "What game are you playing?"

"Game?" Dante repeated, his brows arching. "If I am playing some sort of game, it's for two players only. Newsflash... you aren't my opponent. Oh good! Bekka, come in. Please join us."

Uriel attempted a glance behind him, but only managed to crack his neck. At least it felt better. The rest of him was aching for movement. "Bekka! Are you okay?"

Bekka chuckled. "Why wouldn't I be?" she questioned. "Dante has been taking good care of me." She walked in front of them, bypassing Uriel altogether. Her gaze fell on Veronica. She patted the violin case. "Thank you for retrieving this."

"Bekka, what's going on?!" Veronica shrieked.

Uriel's eyes never left Bekka. He hung on every movement – every word. "Bekka," he whispered. "Why are you doing this?"

Bekka turned to face him. "Because," she replied. She paused long enough to watch a tear fall down his cheek. "I can."

"But-t," Uriel's voice shook, "I love you. We were meant to be together."

Bekka staggered backward, silent.

Chapter Twenty-Four

Veronica's heart raced. She'd put off facing the truth until that moment. A part of her had clung to the hope there was nothing between Bekka and Uriel – that there was a chance he might care about her. That glimmer was extinguished the moment he uttered those words. There was no denying Uriel was the one she had been waiting for. She'd known it instantly. He filled the void she'd dreamed of filling all her life. He also belonged to someone else.

Bekka took in a breath of air and huffed it out again. "You don't love me!" she exclaimed. "You don't even like me."

Veronica alternated her glances between the two. Bekka stood fast, hands on her hips. Uriel, however, wore his heart on his sleeve and it was clearly breaking. Her own wasn't fairing much better, although she hid it from view.

"You know we were meant to be," Uriel whispered. "You know you are my mate. Tell me you feel the same. If I am to die here today, I need to hear your sweet voice pledge your love to me."

"He's lying," Bekka said, looking back at Dante.

"Is he?" Dante asked, raising one brow. He reached out, snatching the case. A single flip of the latch and it was open for all to view.

"It's beautiful," Veronica said.

"You act as if you've never seen it before," Bekka scoffed. "You knew I had it all these years."

"I knew you had a violin passed down through your family," Veronica agreed. "I may have even seen it once or twice, but not this close. It's exquisite."

"Indeed," Dante said. He pulled it from the case, examining every side. "It's a genuine treasure. It may even be the only one left in existence." He raised it up high. His hand came down with authority.

"No!" the girls shrieked in unison. It was too late, though. The violin lay in splintered pieces on the ground.

"Why would you do that?" Bekka asked.

"Relax," Dante ordered, pushing around pieces of wood. "There are far better versions of this instrument in my private collection. I can provide you with a lost Stradivarius, if you so desire. This was a wonderful piece, but its sound wasn't perfect. Ah, here it is." He held up a piece of paper. "This is what you were keeping safe." He put it in his upper suit jacket pocket, patting the outside.

"What was that?" Uriel asked.

"That was a piece of the truth," Dante replied. "Let your sister know I found one. I'm sure it's been driving her crazy;

trying to figure out what the piece she has means. I suppose if anyone other than myself can, it will be her. Now, down to the other issue at hand." His eyes shifted between the two women. "Dean!"

"Yes, sir," Dean replied.

Veronica struggled to see behind her. A man had been in the room the whole time and she had no clue. The whole situation was way over her head. Bekka had turned her back on their friendship. And Dante – she didn't actually know what he was up to, but it probably didn't involve leaving witnesses. She was alone. Her eyes stung. A single glance at Uriel opened the dam. At that point, nothing could have held back the tears.

All her searching had been for naught – every bad date – every wrong swipe of the app. It had all been leading to the moment she met Uriel. He was the one person she'd been looking for and the one person she could never have. He was in love with her best friend. Bekka might have thrown their friendship away, but she wasn't that fickle. If Bekka felt even the tiniest bit for him, there was no choice. She would bury her feelings and step aside. That was the right thing to do – it was the only thing to do.

"Please take Bekka and prepare her for the ceremony," Dante requested, rubbing his mouth using his thumb and forefinger. "We can't afford any mistakes."

"Yes, sir," Dean answered, his hand gripped tightly on Bekka's arm. He yanked her toward the door.

"Ow!" Bekka screamed. "Dante, he's hurting me."

"Go with him," Dante ordered. "Do what he asks, and there won't be any pain involved." He made a shooing motion with his hand.

"No!" Uriel cried. "Bekka. Don't worry! I'll find a way for us to be together again." His pulling and tugging resumed. "Bekka!"

"Save your breath," Dante said. "They are gone." He circled the chairs. "I have to admit, I never took you for the serious type. This is a side of you I didn't know existed. I have to wonder why that is..." He paused, leaning in close to Uriel's ear. "I suppose I'll figure it. An invitation to the festivities might be in order. I'll take my leave of you. Don't bother to get up."

"Very funny," Uriel snapped.

"Someone has to make the jokes," Dante replied. "If it isn't going to be you, I might as well have a go at it. Until later..."

Silence crept in swifter than an airborne virus. There were no words, sounds, or movements. The two simply sat side by side, facing forward, and perfectly still. Waiting was the bane of the curious. Anticipation surrounded them, thickening the air. One wrong thought and suffocation was sure to follow. Still Veronica needed to know – to understand what was happening. If she was going to die, she deserved at least that. Her mouth opened, forming an oval shape, but the words refused to form.

Veronica longed to gaze upon Uriel, but dared not. It would have been far too easy for her own expressions to betray her. The last thing she wanted was for him to take pity on her. She already knew her love was unrequited. She might as well have been waiting in her lawyer's office to have an X-ray. It simply wasn't going to happen.

Chapter Twenty-Five

"It's time for the main event," Dante said, returning. "I have people questioning why I would allow you to attend, when your brother and sister previously ruined our plans. I tend to agree with them."

"So why are you here?" Uriel questioned, a smirk forming in one corner of his mouth.

"Because I have to be sure," Dante replied. "My subordinates have messed things up beyond belief. That leaves me in quite the predicament." He paused, pacing back in forth in front of the prisoners. "Dean!"

"Yes, sir!" Dean replied.

"Take the woman," Dante demanded. "Prepare her for the ceremony as well."

"You want both woman prepared the same way?" Dean asked. "I'm not sure I understand..."

Dante held up his hand, stopping his assistant's words. "It isn't for you to understand. I am telling you what to do.

This is part of cleaning up the mess you made. Follow my orders or there will be consequences."

Dean nodded, untying Veronica's bindings. "Let's go!" he instructed. "Time is short."

"I'm not going anywhere," Veronica shrieked, attempting to pull away from the guard. "I don't know what you are planning on doing, but I don't like the sounds of being prepared."

"Relax," Dante said. "We are simply providing you with a change of clothing for the ceremony to come."

Uriel's gaze lifted to meet Veronica's. There was nothing more he wanted other than to tell her everything was going to be fine, but he couldn't. If he did, it would ruin Plan B. Dante needed to believe that Bekka was the one he loved. The confusion between the two was the only reason his bindings were being removed. Dante wasn't sure which woman was the key. He was only one who could confirm that – he was the only one who knew which of the two was his mate.

His heart wept at the sounds of Veronica's screams, but his exterior never flinched. It had to be that way if there was any chance to save either one of them. Her voice disappeared the moment the door shut.

Dante took a deep breath in through his nostrils and exhaled quickly. "I'm going to release you," he said, pursing his lips together. "I've already taken your guns. Why you chose them out of the arsenal available to you, I'll never know. They are a most vile weapon. A sword is the more gentlemanly choice."

"A sword is your choice," Uriel snapped. "I am not you. I find guns work efficiently in this day and age."

"I suppose you'll be going nuclear next," Dante scoffed.

Uriel laughed. "I'm trying to save the planet, not destroy it."

"You're doing a terrible job." Dante commented.

"And I suppose you are doing better?" Uriel retorted. "Last I heard, you wanted to unleash hell on civilization."

"You and your family presume to know what I am up to," Dante snickered. "None of you have a clue. You think you know all that is good and right. I ask you, though; what if you are wrong?"

"Stop talking in riddles," Uriel demanded. "Just spit it out. You obviously want us to understand something. Why not just tell us?"

"You can lead a horse to water," Dante said, his grin growing.

"Explain it to me," Uriel begged.

"No matter how many times you tell a horse it is drinking water, it won't make a difference," Dante said, "unless two things happen. First the horse has to understand your language, and second it has to believe you."

"Okay," Uriel said. "That makes even less sense. This stuff might work with Gabby, but I'm not a scholar."

"Listen today," Dante said. He pressed a button on a remote and the straps on Uriel's legs let go. "You might learn something useful." he paused, staring at the second button.

"Or something Gabrielle might find useful." His finger came down on the remote.

Uriel thought twice about rushing Dante. That would have accomplished little, though. Instead he merely rubbed the red marks on his wrists where the restraints had been, biding his time. "Tell me why I am not killing you again," he snorted.

"Other than the fact I have your weapons?" Dante questioned. One eyebrow lifted, pulling the corner of his mouth up with it.

"Yeah," Uriel replied. "Other than that." He stood, his hand falling to his side, lightly brushing the rope still attached to his belt. Not taking it was a mistake Dante never should have made.

"Because," Dante replied, "you'd never see either of the women again. I have left instructions to terminate them if I don't show up to the ceremony in five minutes. Do you want to take the chance you'll be able to find them before time runs out?"

Uriel laughed. "I guess not, old man. Lead the way."

"Watch who you are calling old," Dante warned. "Some might take offence to that comment."

Chapter Twenty-Six

Tension grew as the walk progressed. Silence made the situation between the two men even more awkward. Teenagers on a first date had more to say to each other. Anything other than the sound of their own breath, or the clicking of shoes on the tile floor, would have been a welcome distraction.

Uriel's lips puckered, whistling a tune from the past. What song it was eluded him, as did why it came to mind at that moment. He wasn't the type to overthink things. Anything that popped into his head usually came out of his mouth without any consideration.

Dante came to a full stop, slowly turning. His tongue darted out, wetting his lips. They puckered out, tongue pressed against the roof of his mouth. He blew hard, creating a tone slightly lower than his companion's. The two whistles harmonized – a symphony in its own right.

The walk continued, weaving from one hallway to the next in an underground maze. A handful of breadcrumbs wouldn't have been enough to retrace his steps. There was no going back the way they came. That meant the escape route needed a Plan B as well. Until they made it to their final destination, such a plan couldn't be formally finalized, though. That meant winging it from thereon in.

A set of double doors came into view. Their size grew the closer the men came to them. Uriel glanced up at two round brass knockers – a good four feet above his head.

"How do you reach them?" Uriel asked.

Dante chuckled. "That's the first question that comes to mind?" he replied. "Nothing else, really?"

Uriel shrugged his shoulders. "I don't see any handles. With that in mind, I assume it's a knock that does the trick. I suppose we could jump, but that would be a bit awkward, not to mention hilarious to watch a man in a three-piece suit attempt."

"No other questions?" Dante inquired, shaking his head.

"Are we going to stand here all day while you quiz me about what I see or don't see to ask about?" Uriel snickered.

"I suppose not," Dante replied. "I thought you might be curious as to why the doors are so large."

"I assumed you had a troll," Uriel answered, "or another equally large creature, the likes of which I haven't seen in centuries. I still feel opening the doors is more important. Then I'll be able to see firsthand whatever it is on the other side."

"Indeed," Dante agreed. He puckered his lips, whistling the same tune from earlier, but a few octaves higher. The door began to move. "Shall we?"

Uriel chuckled. "The exact tune, huh? There is a reason why it popped into my head then. It's something I have forgotten."

"Most likely," Dante replied. "It wasn't really yours to remember. In a way, I am touched that you did, though. Time to go in. Things are about to start. We need to take our places for the show. You have a front row ticket... standing room only I am afraid. I hope you don't mind."

"Not at all," Uriel answered, eager for a peek at what he was up against. His jaw dropped at the sheer size of the room. "To the altar?"

"If you don't mind," Dante agreed. "Watch your footing crossing the bridge. The pit is warming up for the ceremony."

Uriel's eyes took stock of every inch of the empty room – one bridge over the pit – one hanging cage, swinging slightly overhead – one altar with all the usual fixings for a ceremony of any type, religious or otherwise – one violin, its purpose unknown – one way in or out. A deep red material hung from the ceiling at various intervals, spanning the across the entire room. Life-like giant golden statues, holding equally as shiny weapons formed archways leading to the bridge.

"Who are they?" Uriel questioned. "Their features are so..."

"Real?" Dante asked, arching an eyebrow. "That's because they are, or rather were alive. Their size is the reason for the height of the entrance. These men were Zahare's personal guard... turned to metal after his fall. It is said the keys have the ability to reverse the spell and revert them to flesh once again."

"That's what the blood is for," Uriel mumbled.

"Yes," Dante admitted. "The blood of Nakamire's keys is the only thing that can release them."

"The keys don't open the gates," Uriel muttered. "Zahare's guards do. This is all linked to creation and the brothers' fight."

"Very good," Dante praised. "You are putting your sister to shame. I am surprised she hasn't figured this out yet."

"I don't think she saw the likes of these guys," Uriel replied. "I am sure they would have been mentioned."

"True enough," Dante said.

"Why would Nakamire leave them?" Uriel questioned. "Why not destroy them?"

"Why, indeed," Dante said. "Look at them... each posed as to battle, their weapons pointing up. They were positioned here after being turned to gold. Do you see it?"

"The battle between the brothers is legendary," Uriel replied. "It makes sense their downfall came during a fight."

"Those aren't warrior stances," Dante argued.

"You are saying they were protecting something," Uriel replied. "But what, or rather who?"

"Who, indeed?" Dante replied. "Can you think of no one?"

"They were Zahare's guards," Uriel replied. "It makes sense they were protecting him, I suppose."

"Why would they have to?" Dante asked. He held up one hand. "Don't answer. Mull it over a while. I think you'll find your conclusions most interesting. Right now, we have a ceremony to prepare for. The outfits are hideous, but necessary. I hope you don't mind."

Chapter Twenty-Seven

Uriel felt the cuff lock around his wrist. The opposite side of the chain fastened to a similar hoop style knocker as were on the exterior of the doors. Whistling, however, wasn't going to release him from his new bonds – perhaps that was what the violin was for. His nose scrunched. Itches were nature's form of torture. They always knew when his hands were bound. This one planned on staying for the long haul. He tried to reach the side of his nose to his shoulder. A rub or two would at least take the edge off.

"Is your robe all right?" Dante questioned. "You look uncomfortable."

"Bright red never was my colour," Uriel answered. "It clashes with my hair. I'll survive. What comes next?"

"The women," Dante answered, nodding toward a procession approaching the archway of men.

A thumping began as nothing more than a few beats, growing louder. Uriel attempted to shake off a case of the shivers. They were more than happy to vacate from ears' reach of the eerie noises, in doing so they left behind footprints, though – proof of their existence in the form of goosebumps.

The noise, at its loudest, vibrated the floor and walls. Hundreds of feet had joined together, stomping just outside the oversized entrance – their combined sound mimicking that of a pumping of a heart.

Uriel's gaze fell on the two women, dressed as twins born of darkness. Their all-black dresses reached the ground, veils covering their faces. That was one of Dante's play. Hiding identities was an obvious attempt to confuse. It didn't change a thing. He knew without a shadow of a doubt which was Veronica and which was not. He aimed his line of sight at Bekka, making Dante aware of his knowledge as well.

"Dean," Dante said, greeting his assistant. "I see you managed to prepare them both according to my instructions." He motioned to the two guards escorting each woman to stand back beside two demons, also in attendance. His eyes flickered disappointment. He had hoped not to have to resort to other tests.

"Yes, sir," Dean replied.

"Which is which?" Dante questioned.

"Sir?" Dean replied.

"Which is the key and which is not?" Dante said, raising his voice a few octaves. "I told you before, there is no room for error. Yet, that is all I have seen as of late. I need to know the answer and I need to know now."

"The clan thought it was Bekka," Dean said, his voice shaking. "Then she offered proof it was her friend." He licked his lips.

"I know all this!" Dante exclaimed. "Uriel told us it is Bekka. We go back and forth. I need to know which, though. I am asking you to decide."

"I don't know, sir," Dean admitted.

"You have a fifty percent chance of living," Dante explained. "Choose one or the other. Pick correctly and you live to see another choice. Incorrectly, and you won't have to worry about it..."

"Bekka!" Dean exclaimed.

"What?!" Bekka shrieked. "I told you. I gave you the book that proves I am not the key. I was switched at birth. Veronica is the one."

"Relax," Dante said. "Come here and play a song for me." He held out the violin, winking playfully.

Bekka took his offering. Her hands shook as she rested the instrument under her chin. A deep breath steadied the bow. It fell lightly on the strings, music echoing through the hall.

"Thank you, Bekka," Dante said. "You can return to your spot." He turned his attention to Dean. "It wasn't bad, but I think we can do better. Veronica, please play the same song."

Veronica edged forward. "Why?" she questioned. "What good will me playing the same song do?"

"Play a different one, if you like," Dante suggested. "I simply want to hear you play. It's a matter of life or death – Dean's to be exact."

Veronica exchanged glances with Dean. Her hand trembled as she reached for the instrument. It had been some time since she held a violin for a recital. It had been Bekka's first love. The one thing she vowed she would never do was take something away from her best friend. The first notes came off squeaky. She inhaled deeply, beginning again. Music exploded at twice the volume of Bekka's performance.

The demons shrieked, covering their ears. The unearthly noise shook her soul. If a performance was terrible enough to elicit such a sound from the audience, the musician had no right playing. The bow froze in Veronica's hand, unwilling to make another stroke.

"Continue," Dante ordered. "Finish the song." His fingers tapped on the altar around various daggers and knives.

Veronica pushed on, her bow gripped tightly. The music was no longer light and free. It screamed in pain along with the tortured souls racing for the closed double doors. The demons fell into a trembling heap at their base the moment the performance ended. She moved both violin and bow to one hand.

"You see," Dante said. "Now we know." He glanced back at Uriel. "You put on a good performance. I was almost fooled. There was a smidge of doubt, though. That's when I came up with this test. Veronica is the key. I am sorry, Dean. You chose incorrectly." He picked up a shiny blade.

Dean rushed forward and grabbed a blade of his own. His free hand circled Veronica's waist. The tip pressed into the skin on her neck. "You need her," he said, taking a few steps backward.

"Don't do anything stupid," Dante demanded. "Release the girl and we can talk. I can't help you, if you don't."

"It's too late for that," Dean said. "I'm not stupid. I'm a dead man, no matter what I do." He paused nudging his captive in the ribs. "Open your hand."

Veronica held out her palm. The blade slashed at her flesh, setting free a small crimson river. "Ow!"

"This blood is what you need," Dean said, chuckling. "If I destroy it before you can use it..."

"Hang on there," Uriel said. His hand gripped the chain attached to the wall. He shot a glance at Dante. It wasn't the unbreakable metal. This was regular grade stuff. It crushed beneath his grip.

"Don't move," Dean exclaimed. He held her hand over the pit, blood dripping into the abyss.

"All I want is Bekka," Uriel lied.

"Why would you want her?!" Dean screamed. "I was right, wasn't I? She's the real key. I'll screw you yet, Dante!" He pushed Veronica forward, grabbing Bekka to take her place. The pit behind him burst into flames.

Dante shook his head. "You fool. You've given them blood! Hell's fire will be your undoing. Guards, stop him!" He stepped backward, disappearing into the shadows.

Arrows of fire shot out from the pit, hitting each of the guards through the heart. They turned to ash on the spot. Dean dragged Bekka to the bridge. They staggered from side to side as it shifted and twisted from the heat below. The structure collapsed, sending them both into a fiery grave.

"Bekka!" Veronica screamed.

Uriel's arms encircled her, pulling her back. "It's too late. We have to go."

"There's water," Veronica said. "We can put it out. There's a chance she could be all right."

"It's hell fire," Uriel said. "Water won't extinguish it. Only time will satisfy its rage. We have to go or we'll become ash as well."

Dante had escaped. That meant there was a secret passage. Veronica's knees wobbled. Uriel picked her up and carried her to the back of the room.

"I don't believe it," Uriel muttered.

The door was open. It was only a crack, but open nonetheless. He pushed it with one foot, using his shoulder to catch its weight as they passed through. The other side was a single long hallway. There was no need for a trail of breadcrumbs. This corridor led to only one thing; an elevator.

"Things are looking up," Uriel said.

Veronica didn't answer, her face riddled with despair. Her fingers ran over the violin still tightly gripped in one hand. Being thrown into the supernatural was a hard way for anyone to learn it existed. Even harder when loved ones were lost in the process.

The elevator doors opened. Uriel stood face-to-face with destiny. "Dante," he said. "It was good of you to wait for us."

"It took you long enough," Dante replied.

"Is it a fight you are looking for?" Uriel asked.

"Not at all," Dante replied.

"I don't understand," Uriel admitted. "If you let us go, you are losing. Whose side are you on?"

"My own," Dante replied. "And I'm not losing. There is still one more key. It was always going to come down to the last key. I knew that from the beginning. This one, I guarantee you can't win."

"How can you be so sure?" Uriel asked. "We've managed to surprise you every time so far."

"Yes, that is true," Dante agreed. "However, I know Raphael better than any of you. This is one fight he won't even try to win. He'd rather die himself than admit the truth. You'll see soon enough."

"Why are you doing this?" Uriel asked.

"I'll say it again," Dante replied. "Not everything is as it seems. Take a closer look at what you think you know. I'll have the final pieces in my hands soon. Until then, say hello to the family." He held one hand over his head, whistling his tune. The shadows closed around him.

"What happens now?" Veronica squeaked, her eyelids drooping. Exhaustion was setting in both physically and emotionally.

"I'm going to take you somewhere safe. Somewhere we can get to know each other better," Uriel replied. "It'll take some time for you to recover. There will be some emotional scars, too. I'll be here for you, though... whatever you need."

Veronica nodded, burying her face in his chest.

"Okay then," Uriel said, glancing behind him. "Where did I park?"

Chapter Twenty-Eight

"Who is this?" Michael asked, earning him a swat from Tara. "What?!"

"They've been through an ordeal," Tara complained. "Look at them. At least give them a chance to sit down and relax a minute before you bombard them with questions."

"Her name is Veronica," Uriel explained, leading her to a chair. He pulled it out, nodding that everything was okay. "I think she is still in shock."

"What happened to the other one?" Michael asked. "If he gets two mates, I'm gonna be pissed."

Tara punched him a bit harder. "Don't make me get the roses!" she exclaimed. "I can make them grow extra thorns. I've been practising!"

"Bekka didn't make it," Uriel explained. "They were born on the same day and switched at birth. Everyone thought Bekka was the key." He took the violin from Veronica's grasp, laying it on the table.

"But she wasn't," Gabrielle said. "That's why you didn't feel anything for each other. It was never Bekka."

"It was always Veronica," Uriel said. Her face turned to meet his. "I knew from the moment I laid eyes on her, she was the one." He chuckled. "I have to admit, I thought you both were crazy talking about finding our mates." He pulled a chair beside her.

"Anything interesting happen?" Michael asked. All eyes glared at him. "What? It's a perfectly good question."

Uriel laughed. "Yeah," he said. "We had a run-in with Dante. Things got a little weird. He smashed a violin the dated back to the time of the gods for a scrap of paper. He said to let you know he had that piece, Gabby."

"Great," Gabrielle replied. "I can't solve what all this is about without it. Anything else he wanted me to know?"

"The keys aren't actually the keys," Uriel said.

"Come again?" Michael snorted. "If they aren't the keys then what are we doing?"

"That's where things get a bit weird," Uriel admitted.

"Oh, that's where," Ryder scoffed. "I thought it was weird from the beginning. I guess I was way off base."

"Their blood awakens an ancient set of guards," Uriel explained. "It all connected to the brotherly fight Nakamire and Zahare had. Apparently Zahare had a rather large force of very tall protectors. They were turned into gold while on duty. They control the actual keys."

"You're saying they are the only ones who can open the gates to hell?" Gabrielle asked. "That makes no sense."

"Tell me about it," Uriel replied, rubbing his neck. "A few drops from a cut on her hand and they were spitting hell fire in the shapes of arrows. I guess it wasn't enough to reverse their condition, though."

"That explains why Dante was prepared to drain Tara's body of all its blood," Michael said.

"Thanks for the reminder," Tara scoffed.

"Something's not right," Gabrielle muttered.

"Spill it," Michael ordered. "We are working together now, remember?"

"If the guards were protecting Zahare when their unfortunate demise came about, and they are the only ones who can open the locks," she said, pausing. "They must have been the ones who sealed him inside."

"That isn't how things happened," Michael scoffed. "Nakamire sealed him in, protecting the world from his evil."

"So we were told," Gabrielle said. "None of us were actually there to see what happened."

"You are suggesting everything we know is a lie," Michael barked.

"Not everything," Gabrielle argued. "The players on the board are all the same, but what if the positions were different?"

"That's crazy!" Michael exclaimed. "We have been fighting on behalf of Nakamire for centuries."

"Maybe not," Uriel said. "Dante was talking very cryptically. There was a lot of talk about leading horses to water – not everything is as it seems – take a closer look at what you think you know."

"He's trying to prove Zahare's innocence," Gabrielle blurted out. "That's what he has been up to the whole time."

"Where does that leave us?" Michael asked.

"I don't know," Gabrielle admitted. "Do we throw everything we believe in away at the mere suggestion?"

"What if he's right?" Uriel asked.

"Then we have a problem," Gabrielle replied.

Chapter Twenty-Nine

"You couldn't have thought of a better name?" Veronica asked.

"What's wrong with Big Red?" Uriel asked. "It's rather appropriate, if you ask me." He ran a brush over the side of his horse, while Veronica attended to the other. "Don't go getting used to be spoiled like this. It won't be everyday that you have two people grooming you."

Big Red's tail flickered. He huffed, shaking his head.

"Great," Uriel snickered. "You've only been here a few weeks and he's already making demands."

"I plan on giving him a lot of attention!" Veronica exclaimed. "He deserves it. Besides, you come and go too much. He's been lonely."

"I thought the violin was your thing," Uriel complained. "Now you're a horse whisperer, too..."

"I most certainly am!" Veronica declared, bursting out into laughter.

Uriel sneaked around the front of the horse, planning on a playful side tackle. He reached out; grabbing Veronica's arm at the same moment Big Red's head nudged him forward. They tumbled into a pile.

"Hey!" Veronica complained.

"Hay indeed," Uriel said, picking up and handful and letting it fall again. "Come here." He pulled her on top of his body. "I don't know how I lived before."

"That's pretty corny," Veronica replied.

"I'm serious," Uriel said. "I was going through the motions and didn't even know it until I saw you." He brushed the hair off her face. "I've wasted centuries."

Veronica's lips brushed against his. "We have centuries more to make up for it."

Uriel rolled her over, taking the top spot. "That we do," he said. His lips pressed against hers, before trailing down her neck.

A groan escaped her partly open lips at the touch of his wandering hands, making quick work of the buttons on her blouse. "Big Red is watching," she huffed.

"We'll get him his own filly," Uriel moaned. "Then you'll have your own horse to whisper to."

Her laughter warmed the air. "We should move inside," she said.

"All right," Uriel agreed, "but you can try to explain to him what to do when his girlfriend gets here. Maybe you can read them *Fifty Shades of Hay*."

Veronica's eyes twinkled with pure joy. Love at first sight was one cliché she always hoped was real, but wasn't one hundred percent sure existed – that is until it happened to her. With a world full of millions of people, the odds were against them. Still, they found each other. She was more than happy to follow him anywhere, including inside.

"Glad you two are back," Gabrielle said.

"Why?" Uriel asked. "What happened?"

"Michael got in touch to Raphael," Gabrielle explained. "He's headed home. We need to figure out a position and a plan."

"Does he know anything?" Uriel asked.

"Not yet," Gabrielle admitted. "He'll be here by morning."

"Great," Uriel snorted. "It should be an interesting breakfast. What do you think is going to happen?"

"I don't know," Gabrielle admitted. "We have seen three of Ihenna's favourite things so far: flowers, writings, and music."

"That leaves art," Michael suggested.

Uriel's grin widened. "I suppose we'll have to wait to find out. We'll know more *When the Paint Dries...*"

Author's Message

I hope you enjoyed reading *Hitting the High Note* as much as I did writing it.

I hope you'll pick up *When the Paint Dries* for an epic conclusion to the series. Trust me, you won't want to miss it.

A Four Horsemen Novel Reading Order
Book 1: Flower Shields
Book 2: Drawing Strength From Words
Book 3: Hitting The High Note
Book 4: When the Paint Dries

Until next time... happy reading!

ABOUT THE AUTHOR

C.A. King is the recipient of several awards, including: The Hamilton Spectator Readers' Choice Award for 2017 & 2018 Best Author; The Brant News Readers' Choice Award for 2017 Best Author; Readers' Favorite award in the short story/novella category; the 2017 SIBA Award for Best New Adult; the 2017 SIBA Award for Best Novella; 2018 Readers' Favorite International Book Awards: Gold Medal in the Fiction - Supernatural genre; and 2018 Readers' Favorite International Book Awards: Bronze Medal in the Fiction - New Adult genre

Currently residing in Brantford, Ontario Canada, she lives with her two sons. She began her writing career after the tragic loss of her parents and husband. Redirecting her emotions through writing became therapeutic in her battle with depression and in 2014 she decided to publish some of her works.

Other Titles from C.A. King

The Portal Prophecies

These great titles in C.A. King's The Portal Prophecies series are available now at most online book retailers:

A Keeper's Destiny

A Halloween's Curse

Frost Bitten

Sleeping Sands

Deadly Perceptions

Finding Balance

Volume I (Books 1-3)

Volume II (Books 4-6)

The prophecies are the key to their survival. Can they solve them in time?

Shattering the Effects of Time

Join the Shinning brothers, Jessie, Dezi and Pete as they set out on a quest to save their younger sister. No magic known to them or their friends has ever been able to reverse the grip of time. A few legends, however, exist mentioning ancient items that may hold the key to do exactly that.

This brand new series will take you on a search for the Fountain of Youth and Mermaids; a quest for the Holy Grail; a trip to visit Daryl the mountain guru, in the hunt for the Cinamani Stone; on a search for Ambrosia, the food of the Gods; and other adventures.

Surviving the Sins Series

The prophecies are being rewritten. This time someone is using the seven deadly sins: Lust; Gluttony; Greed; Sloth; Wrath; Envy; and Pride, to unlock an ancient evil. The book falls into Jade's hands to answer destiny's call. Can she survive the sins?

Answering the Call
Pride
Lust
Gluttony
Wrath
Envy
Sloth
Greed

When Leaves Fall: A Different Point of View Story

Ralph wakes up to what others only experience in a nightmare. Chained to a shed, he has no idea where he is, or who his captor is. His memories a blurred at best. As the days press on he finds himself experiencing a roller coaster of feelings. Hunger, thirst and pain become his only companions. Flashbacks of a happier time are all he has to keep him going. As his situation deteriorates, he finds himself doubting the very things he wants most – a family.

When Leaves Fall is a dramatic-thriller with a twist. Keep the tissue box close for the ending.

Tomoiya's Story

A Vampire Tale. She had a secret but she wasn't the only one who had something to hide.

Book I ~ Escape to Darkness

Book II ~ Collecting Tears

Book III~ Coming Soon

Peach Coloured Daisies: A Cursed by the Gods Story

He couldn't die. An ancient curse meant she always did. This time, that was going to change – one way or another.

When Daisy's grandmother, her last living relative, passes away, she doesn't know where to turn. Things go from bad to worse when a local psychic tells her about a curse. Alone and confused, she ends up in front of her college professor's office, ready to cry her heart out in his arms.

Matt Demi might be the son of a God, but he's living the life of a cursed man. He's had to watch the woman he loves die on her twenty-first birthday countless times. Nothing he does seems to be able to affect the outcome. When she shows up at his office scared out of her wits by a psychic's prediction, he vows this time will be different.

With only three days, Matt will need to embrace a side of him he swore off long ago to save her, but will he lose himself in the process?

Miracles Not Included

A heartfelt romantic story about: life; love; loss; and learning to love again. If only life came with instructions and a warning label ~ Miracles Not Included.

****

Chris was born to be a writer. Even the smallest of details couldn't pass without notice, often becoming part of a plot for her next novel. The one thing she never saw coming was her husband's sudden illness.

Jason loved his wife from the moment they met. Nothing could ever change that – nothing except the death sentence he'd been handed – a terminal cancer diagnosis.

His story was ending: Hers was starting a new chapter and more than one miracle was needed to turn the page.

Twisted Tales of a Dead End Street

A paranormal mystery laced with comedic undertones: Twisted Tales of a Dead End Street.

Nine neighbours were invited to the mysterious dinner party at 9 Nine Street. Their host, the owner of the mansion, had more planned for the evening than just roast beef.

When the secret of their quiet street was revealed, everything changed, blurring the lines between the tangible and the paranormal.

Was the number nine the difference between life and death? Would any of them survive long enough to uncover the truth? They would each soon find out this wasn't a simple case of who-done-it so much as one of what was being done and by whom.

Shot Through The Heart: A Faerie Tale

A tale of two worlds – one filled with magic; the other void of it. But what happened to those trapped between the two? Adelia was about to find out...

Magic and structure were the foundations of her existence. Temptation controlled the ability to destroy everything she knew. The world of men held a powerful allure over her heart, waking that which had long been dormant. It enticed her, snagging her in a web of emotions.

A decision had to be made. Was feeling love for the first time worth sacrificing magic and immortality?

Do Not Open Until Halloween

When eighteen year old Caitlin agreed to babysit her eccentric Aunt's two cats and house, she had no idea that Justin was finally going to ask her for a date the same weekend. Torn between family and crush, she chose to take her best friends' suggestion to heart, arranging a small Friday night gathering. Little did she know a fairy was about to crash the party with trouble hot on her wings.

Caitlin will have to dig deep to find even a smidgen of belief in magic or there won't be any hope of saving her new friend from being hunted.

In this young adult fantasy, award-winning author, C.A. King, explores the answer to one of the questions readers have always wanted to ask...

Where do fairies come from?

Welcome to Knollville Series:

Paranormal Detective Mysteries.

Truly Unfortunate

Serendipity's Debt

Hope After Death

From Alice to Malice

Sometimes Love Stinks

What's in a name? Everything when it's laughable.

Gastrella M. Balance was living a never-ending nightmare. For several years, she'd been the butt of jokes about... her butt. Moving to Knollville was a chance for a fresh start. It was a place where no one knew her past, or her name and she was determined to keep both a secret. Her strategy was to stay under the radar and as inconspicuous as possible. That plan, however, went south the first time she laid eyes on Tanner. When he noticed her, too, she couldn't help but hope for a bit of romance, no matter how far fetched it seemed.

*****

Tanner had everything a guy could ask for in his senior year of high school. He had a football in one hand and a pretty girl hanging off the other arm. Being popular and the centre of attention came naturally to him. Taking tests, however, did not and he was desperate to keep that part of his life to himself.

When a series of pranks go awry, they'll both be faced with confronting their personal anxieties. Together, they might have a chance to overcome the odds and survive the year.

Sometimes Love Stinks is a romantic comedy that deals with issues that are both real and difficult. While the main characters in this story are from the mundane world, readers can expect to find the signature supernatural kiss C.A. King adds to all her books.

www.ingramcontent.com/pod-product-compliance
Lightning Source LLC
Chambersburg PA
CBHW031112260626
47172CB00001B/328